Within This Skin

By

Angela Chapman

"Within This Skin" by Angela Chapman, ISBN 978-0-9845362-4-5

Published 2011 by Fire Pit Creek Publishing, 31208 E. Heidelberger Road, Buckner MO 64016 US. ©2011, Angela Chapman. All rights reserved. No part of this publication may be reproduced, stored in a retrieval system, or transmitted in any form or by any means, electronic, mechanical, recording, or otherwise, without the prior permission of Angela Chapman.

www.firepitcreek.com

Edited & Critiqued by: Troy Sawyer

Manufactured in United States of America

Special Dedications:

Ellen DeGeneres: Thank you for taking a stand and speaking out during a time when gays weren't viewed so openly. I believe that you have made a huge impact on the positive way that the homosexual community is now viewed.

Jonna Spencer: You've always been my ideal role model. I always admired the way you would speak so highly of your son and his partner in public...regardless who could hear. When I found out that my son was gay, I knew that you were exactly the kind of mother I wanted to be like!

LGBT Community: I hope all of you can find peace and happiness in your lives.

Special Thanks:

I want to thank my loving mother, Lela Bryant, for raising me not to discriminate against others and for supporting gay rights.

I want to thank my wonderful husband, David Chapman, my daughter, Brittney Bayne, my sister, Candy Myers, and my step-son, Austin Chapman, and all my fans for their support and input on this book.

I want to thank my future son-in-law, Troy Sawyer, for all of his hard work on editing and critiquing. His input was exactly what I needed to complete this book.

And last but not least, I want to thank the one that inspired me to write this book....my amazing son, Brady Jobe.

Chapter One

Sunday, June 1, 2008

As soon as she heard the voice on the other end, Monica's hand slipped from the cell phone. She covered her mouth to muffle the cry from slipping out. The phone crashed on the hardwood floor, and the back cover popped off. She glared at the cell phone as if it had the plague. The tears poured down her cheeks. How long she stood there—she wasn't sure. Her mind raced.

She couldn't believe that it was just yesterday she'd watched Kade, her only son, cross the stage to get his diploma. And how proud she had been when he'd delivered the speech that he'd written, *'As We Move Forward'*. He had talked about all the experiences they had all shared as a class and how they now were going to move forward to follow their dreams. It had been such a touching speech, and there hadn't been a dry eye in the auditorium.

Monica recalled how, at that very moment, she knew she was the luckiest mother in the world to have Kade as a son. He'd accomplished so much his last four years of high school. He earned valedictorian of his class had received several scholarships. He was even voted president of his senior class.

"Omigod, my poor baby," she mumbled under her breath. She shook her head in disbelief.

She glanced toward his choir picture hanging about the piano. He had advanced to state in music and was casted as the lead role in the musical 'Grease'. Her eyes wandered to the paper picture frame, which she never could seem to remember to buy a wood frame for when she went to Wal-Mart. It was a group shot of his track team along with an individual picture of Kade. He had won numerous medals in track the last few years.

Everything a mother would want from a son, Kade had delivered. She wiped at the tears with the sleeve of her blouse. And to think, he already had his whole life planned out—he was to leave in the fall to attend Arizona State University to major in Business and minor in the Performing Arts.

But deep down Monica had known something wasn't right. She had sensed Kade's unhappiness and felt his uneasiness. Even through his joys and smiles, she'd known something was troubling him. Maybe that is what led her to snoop. The distance between them had grown progressively throughout the last couple of years. They used to share everything, but now he was more secretive about his life, his friends, and his whereabouts. Something was going on but she couldn't quite place it—*until now.*

Monica glanced down the hallway toward her bedroom door—thankful that she hadn't woken Wayne when she'd dropped the phone. She hurriedly scooped up the phone and clicked the back on it. She skimmed through her phone records, deleting the last number she'd called.

She was glad Kade and Karmen were both gone for the evening. Her youngest daughter had just turned sixteen a month ago and with school being out for the summer, her curfew had changed to 11:00 p.m. She never came home a minute earlier either.

Monica could never fall asleep until she knew both kids were home safe; another reason Monica was glad she was a teacher and had the summer off. She'd been teaching 8th grade Algebra for the last twenty-five years.

She glanced at the clock on the wall—10:35 p.m. She had no clue what time Kade would be home. He claimed him and some friends were going out to eat and then bowl. But now—she didn't know what to believe any more.

It was about a year ago that Monica started noticing a change in Kade. If he got a cell phone call, he would sneak away to his room, or he would always lock his door when he was on the computer. And he always kept his room locked when he went to school. Monica tried confronting him a few times, but he always alleged nothing was wrong and that he was fine. He always claimed that he just wanted some privacy.

She dropped to the kitchen chair and stared at the phone bill in front of her. She'd been monitoring it for the last few months. There was one particular number that popped up on Kade's bill quite often. Monica hadn't recognized it before. She knew most of his friends' numbers and even had some of them programmed into her own cell phone.

This one number that kept showing up was mostly during the evening hours or on the weekends. She knew, for whatever reason, it was the answer to Kade's sudden secrecy. Her first thought was that it was a girl that she and Wayne probably wouldn't approve of. Maybe even an older woman. She even wondered if the girl could be an atheist, but she dismissed that assumption quickly, knowing Kade was extremely religious and wouldn't even considerate dating someone that wasn't.

She decided to wait until after graduation to push the issue with Kade. She planned to talk to him this evening when he got home, but her impulsive nature got the best of her. She'd waited until Wayne had fallen asleep and then she slipped into the kitchen. She switched her cell phone to hide her number and then dialed the mysterious number. She sighed with relief when she realized it was going to the voice mail. But what she wasn't expecting was the voice on the other end to say, 'Hi, you have reached John. Leave a message, and I will get back with you.'

"John," she repeated. *Why would he be calling John late in the nights? Why would Kade be hiding it from me if something wasn't wrong with this picture,* she asked herself over and over. She suddenly crumbled up the bill and threw it against the patio door. She knew! She knew exactly why—*her son was gay.* It had to be. That was the only logical explanation that there was. She folded her arms onto the table, buried her head into them, and sobbed uncontrollably. She couldn't believe this was happening. After several minutes, she jerked her head up—she had pitied herself for the last five minutes wondering what people would think and how she was going to hide it from Wayne. She hadn't even thought of Kade.

"Oh, Kade, I am so sorry." She cried softly. She had been so consumed with what her family and friends would say—that she hadn't thought about what poor Kade had gone through the last few years.

She suddenly recalled all the cruel gay jokes that Wayne always made. She remembered now that Kade always laughed, but he would never comment. Monica felt a tug on her heart. She could imagine how much his father's jokes had hurt him. And the way Kade's friends would carry on—the names they would call each other and the horrible gay slams!

Her tears increased by the second. Her heart ached for Kade and all the torment he had to have gone through in high school. She knew kids could be so mean.

The more she continued to think about the situation, the more the puzzle pieces started to fit together. It now made sense why the relationship with him and Kelly didn't last. They dated during his sophomore year in school. And as sweet and cute as Kelly was, Monica could tell that Kade just didn't seem interested. They finally broke up but remained friends. He hadn't had a girlfriend since. Although he did escort three or four different ones to the school dances, he considered them just friends. Monica was surprised she hadn't noticed all the signs before since one of her own best friends had been gay. Now looking back, maybe she did see the signs but was just in denial.

She jumped at the sound of the front door opening. She hadn't realized it was already eleven.

Karmen bounced into the kitchen, "Hey, Mom." She kissed her mother on the cheek. "I am early!" She nodded toward the clock on the wall and grinned. It was two minutes till eleven.

Monica quickly stood, rotating her body at an angle so that Karmen couldn't see her swollen eyes. She glanced toward the clock as she walked toward the sink. "Not by much, though." She quickly glanced over her shoulder and smiled to let her daughter know she was playing along. She spun back toward the sink and started running water over the remaining dishes. Unfortunately, that brief second was long enough for Karmen to notice Monica's red eyes.

"You been crying, Mom? Is something wrong?"

"It is nothing, honey. Your dad and I just don't always see eye to eye on things." Monica cringed. She hated lying to her like that—but it was the only thing she could come up with. She couldn't let anyone else find out what she'd found out tonight. Kade would be devastated; and the thought of Wayne finding out sent chills down her spine. She didn't know how he would take it, but more than likely, he wouldn't take it well. He'd never known anyone gay and had no desire to have any friends that were. Monica learned many years ago some things were just better left unsaid with Wayne. If he had his mind made up about something, no one was going to change it.

"Daddy can be so hardcore sometimes. I believe he'd make a better drill sergeant than an accountant. He never listens to anyone else's reasoning! I get mad sometimes too, Mom." She glided over and wrapped her arm around the small of her mother's back. "I'm sorry daddy made you cry."

"It's okay, sweetie. He didn't mean to, and he does feel bad about it now." She squeezed her daughter before pulling away and reaching for a towel to dry her hands. "Anyway, I am going to finish up in here and call it a night." She kissed her daughter on the forehead and shooed her toward the door. "Don't stay up all night either."

"I won't," Karmen rolled her eyes and grinned. "Good night, Mom."

"Night." Monica waited until she heard the bedroom door shut and then snatched the phone bill lying near the patio door. She was thankful that Karmen hadn't seen it, or she would have asked even more questions.

Monica unfolded the paper, pressing the wrinkles out on the table. She hurriedly folded it and stuck it in the hidden compartment in her purse along with the other receipts that she tried to keep hidden from Wayne. He didn't want her spending extra money on the kids. He thought since Kade and Karmen were both working, they should buy all of their own things; Monica felt differently. She knew the kids didn't make much money and had to use most of it on gas and school activities. She didn't think they should have to buy their own clothes as well. When they needed something, she would find a way to get it for them. Besides, she was the one that paid all the bills anyway. Wayne would never know.

Her mind raced back to *John* and her recent phone call. She wondered who he was and how Kade had met him. She fixed a glass of tea, flipped the kitchen light off, and went into the living room to wait for Kade.

She had no clue what she was going to say to him, but she knew she had to try to talk to him. She hoped that somehow she could get him to confess his big secret. She wanted him to know that she would love him no matter what and would stand behind him, regardless! But she had to have answers. She had a very open mind, although she didn't have a clue about being gay in this day and age.

She wondered if she'd done anything wrong in raising him. She had started taking her children to church back when they were early toddlers, and although they didn't go every week, they were still very active with their church. Kade had always been religious and had helped with the local church camp for the last few years. So there was her answer—she knew she couldn't have led him in the wrong direction.

She glanced at the clock on the TV mantel—11:15p.m. Her nails tapped impatiently against her glass. She didn't care if she had to wait all night.

This was going to be the hardest challenge ever. She didn't want to cry or pity her son. She wanted to let him know it was okay and that his decision didn't make him any less of a person. She didn't want him to feel like a failure in life after all he had accomplished. If he thought for a second that he'd disappointed her, it would crush him. She just prayed she could stay strong.

She heard a car door slam—her heart raced. She cleared her throat and straightened in the chair as if she was getting ready to be interviewed for a job. "God, help me please," she mumbled quietly.

***

"Hi, son." Monica held the door open for him and patted his back as he entered.

"What are you still doing up?" Kade asked.

"I don't have to work tomorrow. I can stay up as late as I want, remember?"

"Sure." Kade turned down the hallway. "Good night, Mom."

"What's your hurry? I was hoping we could talk for a bit."

Kade twirled around. "Sure, what's up?"

Monica's mind raced. *This wasn't going well*, she thought. "Can't you sit down and relax a little. You don't have to get up early."

"Sorry, I'm just tired." He flopped down in the overstuffed recliner and pushed the footrest out.

Monica sat across from him on the wooden bench against the wall. She was sure no one would be able to hear them talking. "I was really proud of you yesterday.

Everything happened so fast—I don't even think I told you."

"Sure you did...a dozen times or so." Kade smiled. "I don't mind, though."

"Well, I am proud! You're the best son a mother could have." She stood, strolled to the window, and tightened her robe around her waist. She pretended to be looking up and down the street and then turned back to face Kade. "But I can't help but notice you have changed. It's almost like something is on your mind." She paused. "You know there isn't anything in the world that you could tell me that would make me any less proud than I am right now. I love you unconditionally. You do know that, don't you?"

"Of course I do, Mom. Why do you always suspect something is going on? I am fine. I have just been really busy these last few weeks with graduation and all. I probably seemed a little stand-offish, but I didn't mean anything by it."

"It's not that. It is something I have noticed in the last year. You use to bring your friends over all the time. But now you don't bring anyone, and I don't even know who you hang out with anymore. I just feel like you don't tell me a lot...and you used to tell me everything. We had such a great bond and I miss that." She crossed behind him and gently ran her hand over his hair. "You can confide in me about anything, Kade. You have always been my best friend, you know? And I thought I was yours." She bowed her head, not sure where else to go with the conversation. She didn't want to come out and ask him, but it sure didn't look like he was going to admit anything.

"Is everything okay with you and Dad?"

"Yes, of course." She wasn't sure where that had come from. She didn't know if he was trying to change the subject or if he was being sincere.

"You're just acting strange tonight, Mom."

She threw her hands up in the air. "I just want you to be honest with me. That is all I want." She took a deep breath. "Okay, I am not going to beat around the bush any longer. Who is John?"

Kade's face suddenly paled and when he spoke his voice was faint, "John? What do you know about John?"

"I know his number is on the phone bill a lot, *and* I don't know who he is."

Kade grew angry. "So you are spying on me now? He is just a friend. Have I ever given you any reason not to trust me? I don't believe this!" He stood ready to bound to his room.

"Wait, Kade. I'm not mad. I just want some answers." She motioned him to sit back down. "I know this is none of my business, but I have to know the truth." She hesitated, as she tried to find the right words, "Are you gay?" She held up her hand to quiet him from speaking. "Please hear me out. It doesn't matter to me if you are. You are my son, and I love you so much. I am not going to tell a soul if you are. I just need to know. Please, Kade, be honest with me."

Kade stared quietly out the window as a single tear trickled down his right cheek.

Monica had her answer. He didn't need to say a word. She knew. Anyone that wasn't gay would defend himself in a heartbeat if they weren't. She could see more tears welding up behind his eyelids. He was trying his best not to break.

"Come here, sweetie." She embraced him as he sobbed against her shoulder. "It's okay. We will make it through this."

Kade pulled away from his mom and cleared his throat. "Mom, I can't help it! I don't want to be like this. I have prayed and prayed, but I can't help the way I feel toward other guys. I have been fighting this feeling for the last few years." He exhaled and continued, "I have researched everything about it. I read that it has a lot to do with the genes and some say it's hereditary."

"I was worried I had done something wrong in raising you."

He wrapped his arm around his mother's shoulder. "Of course not. It has nothing to do with that. But many people do believe that, or they believe that men choose to be gay. I don't care what people say." He shrugged his shoulders. "Mom, I would have never chosen this! Others I have talked to agree! But no matter how hard we reject it, pray for it, or try to fix it, there's nothing we can do about it." He sighed. "I want to be normal more than anything in the world. I want a big house with three kids. I want a beautiful wife that I can share my life with. But I would be living a lie!"

He ran his hand through his hair. "Because the truth is—I have had many female friends, and even tried dating a few of them, but there was always something missing. The thought of love, intimacy or a future with any of them was never there. It is not something that I can wrap around my brain, so I have no clue how to express in words to someone who has no idea what this feels like. This all has made me so depressed because I know I will never be able to live a normal life. I'm still trying to deal with all of this, Mom."

"Do you still pray? You haven't given up on God, have you?"

"Of course not; God is all I have to guide me day after day. And I know that God loves me! Since God is the one that made me and he is not ashamed of me—why should I be?" Kade's voice grew angry, "Everyone in the world can look down on gays and make fun of us—but in my heart, I know where I stand with God. He is the only one I need to please in my life—not all the other homophobic hypocrites in this world that call themselves Christians.

"Oh, honey, I am sure not everyone hates gays."

"Mom, there is a lot of them that do! And one of them is my own father."

Monica had briefly thought about how Wayne would react if he found out. But she imagined it was continuously on Kade's mind and that's why he hadn't confided in her. "I am afraid your dad isn't very opened minded and that is unfortunate. I didn't know he was like that for years. I am so sorry, but I don't think we should tell your father about this yet." It broke her heart to see the painful look in his eyes. "I will not let him disown his son, Kade! I will not let that happen. Do you hear me? You haven't done a thing wrong, and you shouldn't be treated like you have."

Another tear fell down Kade's cheek and he caught it with the back of his hand. "I need to go to bed now, Mom. I don't want to talk about this right now."

"Sure, honey." She stood on her tiptoes to kiss his forehead. "It will be okay. I love you."

"Thanks, Mom. And thanks for understanding." He kissed her on the cheek, spun, and hurried down the hallway.

"We will talk more later. It will be okay. I love you," she called out after him. Her mind was spinning and her heart felt like it had been shredded in a million pieces. It was killing her to see her baby boy in so much pain. If only she could take the pain away and give it to herself, she would do it over and over again. There was nothing in the world like seeing one of your children hurting like that. She had held back the tears while she spoke with Kade, and now they slid freely down her cheeks. She thought of what he said about the gay-haters. *How could anyone hate my son?* He was the most loving and giving person she knew. She wouldn't have it—she wouldn't have anyone saying anything negative about her son. She'd fight for him every second.

She was going to start her research tomorrow and learn everything she possible could about homosexuals. She knew at that very moment there was nothing in this would that she wouldn't do to save her son from disgrace.

Chapter Two

Kade stared up at the ceiling. *That was really hard,* he thought. He loved his mom so much and hadn't wanted her to find out the truth because he didn't want to hurt her. But now that she had, he was so relieved. It would be nice not to have to hide it from her anymore. It was so difficult, day after day, pretending you were someone that you weren't. Kids at school were the worst. There wasn't a day that went by that he didn't hear the phrases 'faggot' or 'you're so gay'. It was hard laughing with the guys just so they wouldn't figure you out.

He'd found John on Facebook and had started communicating with him. He was from Olathe, Kansas, just like himself. Kade had hoped there would be some chemistry between them, but after meeting him a few times, he realized there weren't any sparks between them. They did enjoy each other's company, though and slowly became best friends rather than a couple. It was good to have a friend that could relate on the same level, although John was in a much worse situation. He said if his family ever found out about him, they would kick him out and disown him.

Kade suddenly had the urge to share the latest with his friend. He scooped up his cell from the nightstand and texted John.

Hey, you still up?

After a few seconds, Kade's phone beeped back. *Yeah, what's up?*

My mom knows about me.

OMG, is it bad?

No, not at all—she is cool with it.

I am so happy for you. My parents would kill me—literally.

Well my dad doesn't know yet, and he won't be as cool about it as my mom. But my mom isn't going to tell him.

That's cool. Text me when you wake up. You still want to hang out after you get off work tomorrow night.

Yeah, sounds good. Later.

Kade worked at Price Chopper as a bagger and carry-out boy. He'd been there for the last three years and figured he'd work the rest of the summer before going off to college. Tomorrow was a short shift, noon to six.

He placed his cell phone back on the nightstand and rolled over on his side. He closed his eyes and prayed silently. He didn't ask God this time to make him straight. He was going to be okay with it now that his mother had accepted him. It made all the difference in the world having support from his parents; even if it was just one.

He closed his eyes and let the tears hit his pillow. At first, it was just a few, but they increased as hundreds of thoughts raced through his head.

He recalled the day when he first realized he was gay and how confused he'd been. He remembered being in sixth grade and was sitting in the back of the class when Mrs. Duncan called Troy to the front of the room to read his book report. Troy was the most popular kid in the class. He was tall and on the thin side but not too skinny. He wore his black wavy hair long and his eyes were black as coal. He was known for being funny. When he laughed his dimples made all the girls giggle.

Kade remembered staring at him that day and thinking how cute he was. And when Jenny, the prettiest girl in class, was called to the front, Kade hadn't even given her a second glance. He'd thought that it was odd and wondered if he was just jealous of Troy, but he knew that wasn't it. Kade knew there was something wrong—and that something wrong was that he was attracted to Troy. He wasn't supposed to like boys, yet he couldn't control the way he felt. He was ashamed of those feelings and laid awake many nights crying because he knew he was different from the other boys his age. He hid these feelings from everyone and vowed never to tell a soul.

He had only pretended to be like the rest of the guys. He went out for sports, flirted with the girls, and even tried to date a girl in high school. He'd been living a lie the last seven years of his life just so he would fit in with his class. Now he was tired of hiding in the shell he had created. He wanted out, but he knew he wouldn't be accepted in the world where most didn't understand LGBT lifestyle. He prayed that college would be different and he could come out of the closet and be himself.

Kade grabbed a tissue off the nightstand and blew his nose. The first step of coming out was now over. The person he respected the most had accepted him and that meant more to him than anything in the world. His eyes finally grew heavy as he drifted off to sleep.

***

Monday, June 2, 2008

Monica stirred awake and sat up in bed. She rubbed the sleep out of her eyes as she realized it was her dream that had woken her.

It'd seemed so real. It was a holiday of some sort, and they were having a big family dinner. Kade was married to a cute little brunette gal, and they had three children—the cutest little five year old girl along with two big brothers that were spitting images of Kade.

The images from the dream slowly diminished as the recent events from the night before drifted back. Monica's eyes grew cloudy as the reality of finding out her son was gay surfaced. She hadn't even thought of grandchildren. She suddenly realized Kade would never be able to give her grandkids *Why God? Why is this happening to my family,* she thought. Monica assumed that these sort of things happened to other families—ones with serious conflicts going on, such as abusive relationships or drugs and alcohol problems. Maybe even single parent homes—but not from a good mother and father that had always tried to do the right things for their kids!

She quietly stood and glanced toward her sleeping husband to make sure she hadn't stirred him. She carefully grabbed her robe off the chair and slipped it on. She glanced toward the clock—5:10 a.m. Wayne wouldn't be up for another hour.

She silently strolled down the hallway and into the computer room. She waited for the computer to boot up and then Googled searched *gays*. Several porn sites popped up on the screen. She quickly jumped up, shut the door and locked it. All she needed was for her husband to walk in right now. *That would be kind of hard to explain,* she thought.

She quickly retyped *homosexuals and genetics.* She browsed through many of the different sites. Some sites were cruel about the gay lifestyle. Kade had been right. She hadn't realized that there were so many haters out there. It upset her to read some of the comments people wrote—and to think that people hated *her* son—even though they didn't even know him. It seemed so unfair.

One article caught her attention. It was from Live Science Health. The headlines read: 'Mom's Genetics Could Produce Gay Sons.' *At least Wayne will be glad that he's not responsible,* she thought, sarcastically.

The article explained how women have two X chromosomes but only one is functional. The other is inactive due to a process called "methylation." If for some reason one of the X chromosomes is not turned off, then there is too much genetic material, which can lead to a harmful overabundance of proteins. They gave an example of Down syndrome resulting from the presence of an extra copy of chromosome 21.

Monica quickly read over the research studies that had been done that confirmed what the researchers believed.

She read the article several times, letting the new material sink in.

It seemed to make sense but she still wasn't completely convinced. Although she wasn't sure why Kade was gay, the one thing she did know was that he was definitely *born* gay. Kade would never choose to be gay. "What kid would," she mumbled. The tears surfaced once again as she imagined what he must have thought when he realized he was attracted to guys rather than girls. How scared he must have been when he realized that he was different from the other boys.

Monica's heart was heavy. She was overwhelmed with sadness. All she ever really wanted in life was for her children to be safe and happy. Now she wondered *if he'd ever be happy?* And her worst fear: *How could he ever be safe in a world of haters?*

***

Kade pulled his apron off and tossed it in the back seat of his white Cougar. He walked around and inspected his joy ride for any new dings or scratches before hopping behind the steering wheel; a habit he acquired about a year ago from watching too many TV court shows.

He had worked hard and saved his money for a couple of years to purchase a car of his liking, which ended up being a white 2002 white Mercury Cougar. Even though it wasn't new, it was still in great condition for its age. He thought he'd made a wise decision buying the car; he hadn't had any problems with it. It probably helped that he maintenance it on a regular basis, also.

He started the engine and pulled away from the curb. He was glad it had been a short shift at work. The weather was nice, and he just wanted to hang outside.

He'd talked to John earlier in the day, and he'd agreed to go horseback riding with him.

Kade's Uncle Doug and Aunt Sue had a small farm right outside of the city. Kade was allowed to ride the horses anytime he wanted. He rode them every chance he got, rotating shifts with all five horses. His aunt and uncle appreciated Kade exercising the horses for them. They were getting old and restless and didn't ride as much as they used to. Karmen would come with him every once in a while, but she was more into hanging out with her friends.

Kade drove into a less-developed area in the older section of the city. He turned down the street that led to John's house. The houses were run-down and many of them looked vacant. The grass was already starting to get high in many of the yards. He'd only been to John's house a few times and that was only to pick him up when he couldn't find a ride. John didn't own a car and relied a lot on his older sister to drop him off at places. Currently John just mowed lawns, but Kade recalled him saying he had a job lined up with Papa's Pizza Delivery and would start in a few weeks.

Kade pulled up in front of a faded gray house and honked the horn. All the curtains were drawn closed.

He didn't mind picking up John; it was John that didn't like it. He was scared his father might become suspicious with Kade coming by so much.

Kade leaned his head back against the headrest. He was looking forward to the horseback riding. He wasn't worried that John didn't have much experience with horses. He was sure it wouldn't take long for him to learn the ropes.

Kade was just about ready to honk again when the front door opened and an elderly man around fifty-five or sixty years old stepped onto the front porch. He had thinning gray hair and a long wiry beard that hung down to his chest. He wore dirty bib overalls with rips in the knees and an oiled-stained cloth sticking out of the pocket. He reached into the front of his bibs and pulled out a package of Winston cigarettes. He toyed with one between his fingers as he retrieved his lighter. He lit the cigarette and took a long drag while his eyes traveled to Kade's car.

Kade had no doubt that it was John's father. John had warned Kade on how mean his father could be, and by the looks of this guy, he was certain John wasn't lying.

Kade smiled at the man and waved. He was hesitant whether he should get out and introduce himself. But quickly decided against it as the man's eyes narrowed and he stared directly at Kade.

Kade shivered. It was almost as if the man could read every secret that he possessed. It was creepy.

Suddenly, the front door screen slammed and John rushed toward the car, keeping his head bowed. He jumped in the car and threw a gym bag in the backseat. "Let's get out of here!"

Kade was dumbfounded at the whole scenario. Never once did John look toward his father nor did his father speak to him. But as soon as John glanced Kade's way, he quickly understood. "Omigod, John, what happened to your eye?" He meant it more as a statement then he did as a question. He had no doubt who had blackened his eye. "Your father did that to you, didn't he?" Kade glanced one last time at the evil man who was still glaring at them. He pushed on the gas pedal and spun away from the curb.

John waited until they were half-way down the street and glanced back over his shoulder. "He hates me."

"By the looks of it—it should be the other way around! That's a nasty black eye he left you."

"Yeah, I know. But I deserved it." John lowered his eyes to the floor mat.

"I can't imagine you doing anything to deserve that."

"I did. I can't seem to do anything right." John shifted his eyes to the outside of the window. "All I had to get was a gallon of milk, and I couldn't even do that right." He wiped his nose with the sleeve of his shirt as he fought back tears. "I didn't pay any attention to the change the gal handed me back. I should have known to double check it—she *is* new after all." He grunted as if he was disgusted with himself. "When I got home I was five dollars short!"

"So? It was a mistake," Kade blurted out.

"Yeah I know! But my dad's money is hard to come by, and he wasn't happy with me at all."

"John, I can't believe you got hit for that. That is just wrong. Does he do this to you often?"

"Yeah, but I usually deserve it."

Kade was getting angrier by the second. It was bad enough that John's father hit him, but even worse that John actually believed it was okay and that he deserved it. "No one deserves to get hit or beat in any way, John. That is just wrong what your father did." He glanced toward John. "What about your mom? Won't she help you when he does these things to you?"

"Are you kidding? She knows better unless she wants a beating herself! She's been hit far more times than I have."

"Oh, wow," Kade shook his head in disbelief. "And your sister?"

"Not so much. She doesn't seem to get on his nerves like mom and I do. Besides she's always away with her boyfriend anyway. She says she may be getting married soon."

"Are you close to your sister? Maybe you could go live with her after she gets her own place," Kade suggested.

"No, not really. She doesn't know about me either." John cracked the window open and flipped his bubble gum out. "I think we were too many years apart to have a close relationship." He stared back out the window. "I wish we were, though."

"I don't know what to say. I'm sorry you have to go through that. Anytime you need me to come and pick you up, just give me a call."

"Thanks and don't worry about it. It's no big deal. I am sure I'm not the only messed up guy!"

"Don't say that—it's not true." Kade pulled into the gravel driveway leading to his uncle and aunt's house. "You know what?" His eyes lit up. "You are going to love where we are going horseback riding today. It will take your mind off everything!" Kade hoped he could cheer John up with a ride down to the creek.

"I am sure it will be fun, although I might fall off a few times." John laughed. "I *am* an amateur, you know."

"These horses are so tame—you won't fall, I promise." Kade pulled up to the barn and parked. The next fifteen minutes were spent saddling the horses, and Kade explaining all the riding techniques.

Kade gave John the tamest horse they had. Scarlett was an older quarter horse that moved a little slower than the others and was extremely gentle.

Kade climbed upon his own horse, Maggie Mae, and motioned for John to follow. Maggie Mae was usually gentle too, but every once in a while she'd get a little stubborn and decide to be ornery.

They rode silently for the next fifteen minutes through the thick woods.

"Damn horse! Won't go the way I am telling it to!" John shouted ahead at Kade.

Kade glanced over his shoulder and laughed at the sight of John trying to get Scarlett around a sticker bush. "We are almost there." He yelled toward Scarlett, "Come on, girl. Let's go."

Scarlett immediately obeyed Kade's command and went around the bush.

"That's impressive!" John laughed.

"She is just used to me riding her. She will get used to you." After a few minutes, Kade pointed to the creek ahead. "There it is."

Up ahead was the most beautiful scenery that Kade had ever witness. He loved coming to this spot. The area surrounding the creek was absolutely breathtaking. The abundance of sunflowers let off a bright, golden glow that made the boys' eyes wince at just the sight of them. The green trees, full of leaves, left large patches of shade that any dreamer would love to lie underneath. The running waterfall was so clear you could bathe in it, and the sun beating down on the rocks around it made them sparkle like diamonds.

"Wow," John gasped. "This is awesome. It looks like something out of a picture book."

"I know. I love it here," Kade agreed.

They slid off of the horses, led them to the creek to drink, and tied them to a nearby tree.

Kade led John up to the waterfall and they carefully climbed on the flat rocks surrounding it. Kade moved toward the edge of the rock and lowered himself into a sitting position. He threw his legs over the edge so they were dangling next to the falling water.

John followed. "Wow, how amazing is this? I have never experienced anything like this before!"

"I know. I spend a lot of time here. We can take off our shoes and go below and wade in it too."

John grew silent as his eyes traveled around the area, soaking in the scenery. "Wow, I wish I could stay here forever," he said, full of emotion.

Kade had never seen John look so sad. "Is everything else okay? Are you just upset about your dad?"

After a long silence John finally spoke, "I am going to have to try to lead a straight life, and it is going to be so hard."

"What do you mean?" Kade asked.

"I can never live a gay life. My family won't accept it, so I have no choice but to pretend I am straight." His eyes grew misty. "I don't want to be gay, Kade. I want to be normal so bad." John stared at the waterfall as if in a trance. "I want my father to be proud of me. He would never be proud of a gay son."

"It is not your fault," Kade added. "You can't help who you are any more than I can help who I am. You have to accept yourself and not be ashamed. You can't go through life pretending to be someone that you're not. You will never be happy if you do."

"I can't help it." Suddenly tears were streaming down John's face. "Sometimes I don't even want to live." John cleared his throat and stared toward the waterfall. "I wished I had this place to come to when I'm upset."

"I'm sorry you feel that way." Kade felt so bad for John. "And you can come up here with me anytime you want."

Kade wasn't sure what to think of John's confession. At first, he too had spent a lot of time feeling sorry for himself, but he'd gotten over it and decided to accept his own faith. He started working on building his other strengths to make him a better person. He was proud of all the accomplishments that he had achieved so far.

He had never taken the time to think about other gays and how they coped. This was clearly an eye-opener for him and his heart ached for John. It was sad to know his friend felt so low and alone in this world. Maybe this was another one of God's plans. Maybe he was supposed to help John see the brighter light. He wasn't sure how he was going to do it, but he was up for the challenge. He had to somehow convince his friend that he was worthy. He knew this wasn't going to be an easy task, but he had to try!

"Come to my house tomorrow night for dinner. I want you to meet my mom," Kade blurted out without thinking. He suddenly realized his father would be home and wished he would have thought things through first. Kade didn't like to stereotype, but it was obvious to the eye that John was gay. He wished he could take back his invite, but it was too late now.

Kade cringed—he knew tomorrow could be a disaster and possibly one of the worse days in his life!

Chapter Three

Tuesday, June 3, 2008

Monica sipped her coffee while keeping her eyes glued to the front entrance of the café. She was supposed to meet her friend Crystal at 9:00 a.m., and it was now 9:10 a.m. She wasn't worried, though, as it was normal for Crystal to be late. She was even late to her own wedding twenty years ago. Monica had been her maid of honor and couldn't believe the whole wedding party was there before Crystal ever showed up. It gave Rick a scare too. He thought for a second his bride was going to stand him up. The memory made Monica grin.

She'd decided to share the latest news with Crystal. She was positive she wouldn't repeat anything because Crystal's own brother was gay.

Monica covered her mouth as a yawn silently escaped. She hadn't slept but a few hours in the last couple of nights. It had been an emotional roller coaster. She couldn't stop thinking about Kade being gay. It was on her mind every waking moment. But that wasn't the only thing bothering her. It was the lifestyle in general. She couldn't stop thinking about their lives and how they coped day after day. *And what about the kids in school and all of the peer pressure!* It had to be awful to be gay and try to hide it in high school.

Monica had devoted her attention the previous day and half the previous night on the computer researching everything she could possibly learn about the LGBT community. The most interesting was the religious views that most people conceive about gays. She'd been just as guilty in the past. She'd grew up believing whatever she was told—that gays *choose* their sexual orientation and that according to Leviticus in the Bible they would go straight to Hell! At the time she had no reason to doubt anyone, and she really didn't care enough to explore the truth herself. But now she had a reason and after all the research, she thought that statement couldn't be further from the truth. *Both verses in Leviticus refer to heterosexuals not homosexuals. No hint at sexual orientation or homosexuality was even applied.* Another preacher wrote how using Leviticus to condemn and reject homosexuals is hypocritical selective use of the Bible. *No one in today's world tries to keep the laws in Leviticus—such as: all unclean animals are forbidden as food including rabbits, pigs, oysters, shrimp, lobster and others that are called 'abomination'. And what about the law that declares a woman unclean for 33 days after giving birth to a boy and 66 days after giving birth to a girl?* Monica couldn't believe some of the laws she read. She was certain most people didn't even try to keep these laws and many probably didn't even know about them.

She had learned more in the last 24 hours than she had her whole life about homosexuality and its lack of presence in the Bible because now she *wanted* to learn.

She was convinced that most of the haters in the world hadn't even done any research on the issue. They had probably just heard other people talk and then casted the views as their own.

She was happy to learn about an organization called PFLAG. It was for parents that support the LGBT community. There was a meeting in Kansas City on Thursday night that she was hoping to attend.

She suddenly spotted Crystal rushing through the double doors and waved at her.

Crystal slid into the booth opposite of Monica. "I'm so sorry I am late. I took Justin to baseball practice. And would you believe that it wasn't ten minutes, and he was calling because he'd grabbed Sara's ball glove instead of his own." She flipped her coffee cup over as the waiter approached the table. "Yes, please! I desperately need some caffeine!"

The young man chuckled while pouring the coffee. "I'll be back shortly to get you ladies' order."

"Thank you," Monica replied.

The man disappeared behind the corner.

Crystal immediately continued, "So I had to run his glove out to him. What is it with twelve-year olds forgetting everything anymore?" She rolled her eyes.

"Well, I hate to be the one to break the bad news, but it doesn't get any better either. They are worse in high school." Monica giggled. "You're just starting."

"Thanks," she sighed. "We were never like that, were we?" Crystal tossed her head back and laughed. "Hell, I can remember forgetting my lunch money once my freshmen year, and I just went without lunch. I didn't have a cell phone to call my mom to bring me some money. Wouldn't have mattered anyway—Mom wouldn't have done it!"

"I bet you never forgot your lunch money again!" Monica smiled.

"You're right. I didn't. Funny....isn't it?"

"I know. I think parents were smarter back in the day." Monica instantly thought of Kade. "I take that back. I don't think parents were very smart at all back then. Take your brother, Jim, for example. I bet your parents had no clue that he was gay. And probably didn't know a thing about homosexuals when they found out either."

The waiter approached the table and the girls quickly placed their breakfast order.

After the waiter left the table, Crystal replied. "I still don't think my parents know about Jim."

"What? You're kidding?" Monica was shocked. Jim had to be over thirty-five years old.

"Well, maybe they do, but it has never been brought up. My parents are so old school that I'm not sure how they would react."

"Yeah, I'm finding that out. It is mostly the older generation that has a hard time with homosexual issues." Monica shook her head. "And they are supposed to be the ones to influence our younger ones?"

"Why the sudden interest?" Crystal asked, puzzled.

Monica brought the cup back up to her lips and sipped. "I just found out that Kade is gay." She didn't whisper it or pretend it was a disease. She said it loud enough that the older couple across the aisle turned to stare. It was just the reaction she thought she would get, and it angered her.

"Kade?" Crystal gasped. "I would have never guessed. Wow, that's a shocker." She paused. "Monica, I don't know what to say! I hope it isn't bothering you too bad?" She paused. "I mean I am sure it does. But, really, it is no big deal."

"I know that now, but I have to admit that I was pretty traumatized when I first found out."

"Well, that's understandable." Crystal leaned back in the booth while the waiter set their food on the table.

Monica grew silent. Her mind raced as she stuffed a spoonful of egg into her mouth. She wanted to ask Crystal a favor. It was something that she'd come up with while driving to the café this morning, but she wasn't quite sure what Crystal would think.

After several moments of silent eating, Monica spoke, "I want to help Kade and all the others who are struggling with the same issue."

"Sure you do. I don't blame you. But how?" Crystal asked.

"I am not really sure yet. But I do know the first thing I need to do."

"What?" Crystal dabbed her lips with her napkin.

"I need to know what it is like to be gay. I want to personally experience what Kade has gone through these past few years. I can't help him or others until I know exactly how they feel."

"That's impossible. I know you mean well, Monica. But..."

Monica interrupted, "Oh, but there is a way, and I need your help."

"Okay," Crystal shrugged. "You know if there is a way for me to help, I will."

Monica laughed. "You better wait to hear what it is before you agree." She finished chewing, placed the napkin in her plate, and pushed it away. "I want you to be a lesbian with me."

Crystal's sudden reaction caused her to spit coffee down her shirt. "What?" She laughed as she wiped the coffee off

34

of her blouse. "You can't be serious?" She set the cup down. "Have you lost your marbles? You can't make yourself gay, silly." She giggled. "And as much as I love you, I am not at all interested in you that way! Sorry, honey."

"Very funny. Okay, make fun of me, but I am being serious. I want us to go out in public and pretend we are lesbians. I want to see how we are treated and the reaction we get from other people." Monica stared pleadingly at her friend.

Crystal's eyes widened. "You are serious, aren't you?"

"Very much so! This would mean the world to me if you would help me out. Please, Crystal, you won't be doing it just for me but for Jim and all the others out there."

Crystal shook her head. "I don't see how this is going to help Jim or Kade. But you know what, if it means so much to you, I will do it." She laughed. "Hell, I need some excitement back in my life anyway. This sure will take the boring out of married life. You set up a plan and let me know when, and you can count on me."

"Thank you, Crystal. I owe you!" Monica picked up Crystal's ticket and handed the waiter her debit card.

Crystal giggled. "I still can't believe I am agreeing to this."

Monica paid their bill and told Crystal she'd be getting a hold of her soon. She was so excited that Crystal had agreed. She wasn't quite sure if she would or not.

Monica couldn't wait to get home and start planning her next escapade. She'd decided not to tell Kade about her plan. She didn't think he would understand and might think she was a little crazy. Maybe she was getting a little carried away, but if she could help a few people see differently, then it was worth it!

*** *

Monica was totally surprised that Kade had asked John for dinner. She didn't mind but thought it could be sort of risky if Kade didn't want his father to find out.

She pulled the meatloaf out of the oven and glanced at the clock on the stove. It was 6:20 p.m.—which meant she had less than ten minutes to get everything prepared before they arrived. She finished slicing the meatloaf and set it next to the mashed potatoes on the table. She went back to retrieve the hot rolls out of the oven. Her stomach did a somersault, confirming the nervousness she was feeling.

Wayne entered the kitchen. "I smell some good cooking." He glanced at the food on the table and the cake on the counter "Special occasion? I didn't miss our anniversary, did I?" He smiled.

Monica knew he was poking fun. "Kade is bringing a friend for dinner and since it has been so long since the kids have invited anyone over for dinner, I thought I'd make a cake too."

"Oh, I see. Well that's unusual. A girl?"

Monica cringed. "Umm... no. Just a friend."

The front door screen slammed; Monica knew that Kade was home. "Perfect timing," she called out. "It's ready."

Kade hesitantly entered the kitchen "Mom...Dad...this is John. He is a friend of mine from work."

"Hi, thanks for having me over," John said softly.

Monica knew Kade was lying about where he'd met John. She extended her hand. "You're very welcome. Nice to meet you, John." She glanced toward Wayne. He had a surprised look on his face, and she wondered if he could already tell that John was gay.

36

Wayne briefly shook hands with John. "Hello." He spun back toward the table, pulled out a chair, and sat down.

Monica was shocked at his rude behavior. She was sure now that he had sensed John's 'secret'.

It was no surprise to anybody that John was gay. Monica's heart sank deeper. She could only imagine the hell he must go through trying to cover it up.

"Have a seat guys and eat up." She reached for the pitcher of tea on the counter and placed it in the center of table. "Help yourself to everything."

Monica thought John was a little on the shy side. He was short, probably not over 5'7" and was a little too thin. He wore his brown hair short and a really thin mustache curled around his upper lip. Monica guessed he'd tried everything to cover up his identity. She wondered if his parents knew about him.

"Where's Karm?" Kade asked.

The front door opened and shut.

"I believe that's her now." Monica called into the living room. "Karm, in here. Dinner is ready."

Karmen threw her purse on the floor. "I'm starving!" She quickly noticed John. "Oh, hi."

"This is John" Kade nodded toward Karmen. "My sister, Karmen."

John smiled warmly. "Hi, Karmen. I have a cousin named Karmen. Pretty name."

"Why, thanks." She glanced toward the food on his plate. "You're in for a good treat. My mom is a good cook."

"Oh, I know. I tried the meatloaf already and it is amazing." John smiled at Monica.

"Well, thank you." She glanced toward Wayne; his head was bowed over his food. "Everything taste okay to you, honey?"

"It's fine." He shoved a bite of meatloaf into his mouth and chewed silently.

Monica hated the way he was acting toward Kade's guest. She was embarrassed and it angered her to see him act so childish.

Except for Wayne's unsociable behavior, the rest of the dinner went smoothly. Karmen and John hit it off well and talked about some new reality show on TV while they ate. The food disappeared just as fast as it was put on the table; and Monica couldn't be more satisfied; she loathed leftovers.

It wasn't until later after John had left and the dishes were all done that Wayne decided to comment on the earlier events. He'd spent most of the evening working in the garage.

Wayne washed his hands and glanced around the room. "What? Did Kade's little fairy friend finally leave?"

Monica swallowed, trying to control her anger. She glanced toward the living room, hoping Kade hadn't heard his father's comment. "John's a very nice guy. And you shouldn't call him that."

"Oh come on—he is as queer as they come! And what's Kade doing hanging around with him?"

Monica bit her tongue. *How dare him!*

Wayne yelled into the living room. "Hey Kade, what the hell you doing hanging out with a fag?"

"Shut up!" Monica yelled.

Kade appeared at the door. He looked devastated. "That's not fair, Dad. John's a good friend of mine."

Wayne snorted. "Those aren't the kind of friends you need." He snickered. "Lord, I hope you don't come home wearing a dress next."

"Wayne, shut up right now! I mean it," Monica shouted.

"Come on, Monica, you had to be able to tell he's gay," Wayne twisted a cap off a Budweiser and tossed it in the trash.

"It doesn't matter to me what his sexual orientation is. It is none of my business and it is none of yours!" Monica spat.

Karmen entered the kitchen. "What is going on in here?"

Kade glared at his father. "Dad's a shallow person that's all!" He spun on his heels and marched to his room.

The look on Kade's face would be etched into Monica's soul for the rest of her life. The man Kade had always respected and loved had just broken his heart and crushed his self-esteem. Despite how she thought he might have reacted to John, she would have never guessed it would end like this. How dare him to think that he is better than any other person in this world. How could she have stayed with a man like that all of these years?

"I guess I came in at the wrong time." Karmen backed down the hallway. "I'm going to my room too."

Monica waited until she heard Karmen's door shut. "You are the most arrogant, conceited man I know. And I will not allow you to talk like that about our son!" *Crap,* she thought. It was too late. She'd already said it! Those weren't the words she'd intended.

"Who was talking about our son?"

Monica quickly tried to back paddle, "I mean to Kade's friend."

"That almost sounded like you were implying our son was gay?" Wayne brought the bottle to his lips and guzzled all the beer down in one swallow. "Please tell me that isn't what you meant?"

Monica was speechless. If she wasn't ashamed of her son being gay, then she needed to defend him and stand up to anyone that got in her way; she might as well get the worst one over with. She didn't know if Kade would forgive her for her slip up, but it was too late now. "It doesn't matter if he is. That doesn't make him any less of a person. He is a remarkable young man that I will always love regardless of his sexual orientation, and you should too."

Wayne grabbed another beer out of the fridge. "You're shitting me, right?" He took a swallow and grew quiet. Suddenly he flung the beer across the room. It hit the wall and shattered—beer and glass splattering everywhere. "No fucking way am I going to have a queer son."

"Stop it. He will hear you!"

"Oh he is going to hear me, alright." Wayne leaned into the hallway and shouted. "Kade, get your ass out here now."

Monica darted in front of Wayne. "No, you leave him alone. Don't you dare say anything to him. So help me Wayne, I will never speak to you again."

Kade opened his door. "What now?"

Wayne glared at his son for, what seemed like, forever. The veins in his neck were bulging and his cheeks were scarlet red. "I want the truth! Are you a faggot?"

That was all Monica could tolerate. She shoved Wayne out of her way. "Go to hell, you bastard." She gently pushed Kade into his room. She slammed the door shut and locked it.

"Mom, it is okay. I was expecting this out of dad. I am not shocked at all."

"Over my dead body is anyone going to talk to you like you're trash! To hell with everyone!" Monica couldn't control the tears any longer. "I had no intentions of saying anything—it just came out. I am so sorry!"

"It's okay. I knew it was a risk bringing John here. Oh well, Dad was bound to find out sooner or later." Kade let the tears flow freely down his own cheeks.

Monica's sobs continued. "It just isn't fair. This is so unfair to you, Kade. I am so sorry!" She wrapped her arms around his neck and sobbed into his shoulder. "My poor baby." She caressed his back as she did when he was an infant. "I am going to make things better...somehow. I promise you, son. I am going to somehow make this world a better place for you if it is the last thing I ever do."

Chapter Four

Monday, June 9, 2008

The last five days had been a nightmare for Monica. She didn't remember ever fighting so much with Wayne before. He just didn't get it, and he didn't want to listen to anything she had to say. He had his mind made up the way he believed, and he wasn't going to let anyone change it.

He avoided Kade all together. It ripped at Monica's heart to see the way he was treating him. No one should ever be treated so badly for something that they couldn't help. Monica believed it wasn't any different if their son was handicapped. Would Wayne shun him then and look down on him for something he couldn't help? Monica couldn't believe anyone could be that shallow, let alone her very own husband.

All last week, he'd come home late from work and didn't eat supper, claiming he'd eaten at the office. Monica soon realized the less conversation they had, the less they would fight. She tried a few times to change the subject, but it always led back to Kade and the fight would start over.

She couldn't live this way, knowing her own husband had disowned their son. She stared at the front door, waiting patiently for Wayne to walk through it. She knew what she had to do. When her kids were born, she vowed she'd always protect them, no matter what. It is just what a mother does.

Monica was going to tell Wayne she thought they should get a divorce. She couldn't go on living with him, knowing how he truly felt about Kade. She couldn't love someone that was so totally set against trying to understand the unknown; especially when it came to family.

She had opened her mind and researched until she understood the topic more. Why couldn't he? *Sometimes in life, it takes an unusual situation for people to learn the truth. To get more educated, though, you have to be willing to learn.* And Wayne's own stubbornness wouldn't allow it.

The front door opened and Wayne stepped into the room. He quickly wiped his feet on the doormat before looking up and meeting Monica's gaze. For once, Monica was glad both kids were not at home. This would be hard enough as it was.

"Hi," He sat his briefcase down. "I've already eaten."

"We need to talk, Wayne." Monica stood and cross the room to the window.

Wayne crossed to the sofa and plopped down. "Sure. What's up?"

She spun around to face him. "I don't think this is going to work anymore."

"What?" Wayne asked, puzzled.

"Me and you. I don't think I can stay married to you any longer." She hesitated. "Nor do I want to," she stated firmly. "We are too different in the way we believe and think. We will never come to an agreement over Kade. I can't live with you knowing how you feel about our son."

"Just like that—it's over? All these years...." He stood and shrugged. "Okay, if that's what you want. I will pack up tonight and go stay with my mother until I find something else." He turned to leave but spun back around. "I do love Kade, and I always will, but I can't accept his life style. One day I hope he will change and then I can be a father to him again, but until then—he is not *my* son."

Monica wanted to scream at him but what was the point. How could she have ever been in love with him? She knew he was entitled to his opinion, no matter how disappointing it was.

"Please do not make Kade feel like this is his fault. I want a divorce for my own reasons, and I don't want the kids to think otherwise," she said.

"Whatever you want." Wayne shrugged. "I don't want the house or anything. You can have it all." He marched halfway down the hall and spun back. "I just need some time alone to deal with all of this. This was quite a blow for me to handle."

"I know," Monica said softly. "And thank you for understanding why we can't be together anymore."

"I hate throwing everything away that we had, but I totally have to agree with you. I don't see any other way to make things work at this point."

Monica fought back the tears. Part of her would always love him no matter how much she hated his narrow-minded theories. "I will wait and tell the kids after you leave unless you'd rather tell them?"

"No, you were always better at words than me. I will let you handle it." He glanced toward the floor briefly and then his eyes met hers. "I'm really sorry for everything. I can't help the way I feel."

"I know. And I can't help the way I feel either," Monica stated.

He turned and continued down the hall.

Wow, she thought. *That was easy.* She thought he'd be a little bit more challenging and try to talk her out of it. She imagined deep down she was hoping he'd come to his senses and beg her not to divorce him and admit that he'd been wrong about Kade.

Monica listened as Wayne opened drawers and closets. He hadn't wasted any time starting to pack. The tears were building up behind her eyelids, and she struggled not to release them. She couldn't let him see her cry.

She quietly hid in the computer room while he finished packing.

After a while, Wayne tapped on the door. "I'm going. I'll be back this weekend to get all my stuff out of the garage."

"Okay," she said, disappointed that he hadn't even bothered to open the door to tell her goodbye. She'd often wondered if his love for her had dwindled down; now she was sure it had.

It wasn't until she heard the front door slam and his car leave the driveway that she let the tears fall. She didn't know how long she cried, but it continued on until she'd almost drunk a whole bottle of wine. *How was I ever going to tell Kade and Karmen?*

***

Later: 10:15 P.M.

It was just after ten when Kade got home. He'd swung by earlier and picked John up after he got off work and they'd gone horseback riding. It was John's request this time. He claimed it was an escape from Hell for him. Regardless, Kade didn't mind. He'd ride every day if he had the time.

The house was quiet when he came in, which was unusual. He knew Karmen wouldn't be home yet because her curfew wasn't until eleven, but he thought his mom might be waiting up on him like she usually did. But the living room was dark.

"Mom, you here?" he called out.

He noticed his dad's car wasn't in the driveway, but had assumed it was in the garage. He sometimes pulled it in there if he thought it was going to storm.

Kade's stomach churned—it still hurt the way his father had been giving him the silent treatment. He had once hoped that he'd never disappoint his mom and dad.

Monica appeared in the doorway. "Hi, honey. How was your evening?" She set the near empty bottle of wine on the table.

Kade noticed immediately that she'd been drinking and crying. "You okay, Mom?"

"I'm fine." She hesitated. "I have some disturbing news for you and your sister," she said.

"Is it dad? Is he okay?"

Monica hesitated. "Yeah, he's okay." She picked up the empty glass and poured the rest of the wine in it. She

46

brought it to her lips and took a sip. "There is no easy way to tell you this. Your father and I are getting a divorce."

"What? Why?" Suddenly it hit him. "Oh, I get it. It is because of me, right?" He couldn't believe this was happening.

"No, of course it's not because of you. Your father and I have been having problems for a while."

"I don't believe you, Mom." The tears surfaced. "You never lied to me before. Please don't start now." His words must have hit home because she suddenly grew quiet. "Mom, it's okay. You don't have to keep protecting me. As much as it hurts, I know that Dad can't accept that I am gay."

"I'm so sorry, Kade." She moved toward him and wrapped her arm around his shoulder.

"I can accept the fact that Dad can't accept me the way I am, but I can't accept the fact that I'm the reason for you and him breaking up."

"Kade, you can't blame yourself for this. This is something that has been developing for a while. I think your father has been ready to leave me for some time. He just needed a push and this was it."

"It isn't fair! I'm sorry!" Tears slid down his cheeks. "Sometimes I wish I was never born." He spun and hurried down the hall. He couldn't believe the chaos he'd created.

"Kade, wait! Come back!"

"I need some time alone, Mom. Just give me some space, please."

"Okay, sure. But I will always be here for you."

"I know you will and thank you." He tried to smile through the tears. "I love you, Mom," he said before opening the door to his room."

"I love you too, son."

As soon as he was behind the closed door, the sobs escalated. He hadn't cried like this since he was five years old and the neighborhood boy had broken his batman car.

He fell face first onto his bed. Crying made him feel weak, so sometimes he'd refuse to let go. But now he just couldn't hold back any more. He knew he'd always blame himself for his parents' divorce. He'd never meant to cause this much trouble or pain to anyone. If he could change the way he was, he'd do it in a heartbeat. Why was that so hard for people to understand? This wasn't the life he chose but the life he was given. Nobody wants to be gay, but you can't hate yourself for it either. Kade truly believe that God had a plan for him, although he wasn't quite sure what it was yet.

Kade flipped over on his back and stared up at the ceiling. He thought about all the blogs he'd read on the Internet. Many people just assume gays are just about the sex. They misinterpret the meaning of the bible and automatically go for the evil aspect. They don't, however, try to understand that gay people are just like everyone else. They want to fall in love, get married, and have a family too.

Kade squeezed his eyes shut. *Why God? Why do people condemn me for who I am and they don't even know me? Why are the people in this world so narrow-minded? Why can't they open up their hearts and accept everyone that you have created.* Kade's tears oozed silently down his cheeks. *Please, God, hear my prayers. I need you.*

***

Thursday, June 12, 2008

Monica spotted an empty spot right in front of the building and pulled her Matrix into the vacant area. She glanced at her watch, realizing she had plenty of time to spare. She was attending her second PFLAG meeting and she had ten minutes before it started.

She rolled down the window and retrieved her purse from the floor. She learned so much last week at the meeting; she was glad she'd come back tonight. She also met some of the nicest, open-minded people too. She realized there were a lot of parents in the same boat she was in, and they all agreed that their children needed all the support they could get.

Monica dug in her purse for her lipstick. She pulled down her visor mirror and applied the bright red to her lips.

"Excuse me, Ma'am," a plump, elderly lady said loudly.

Monica jumped. The woman at her window startled her.

"I'm sorry, Ma'am. I didn't mean to scare you."

Monica laughed. "That you did—but it's okay." She opened her car door and rolled up the window before climbing out. "May I help you with something?"

"Yes, Ma'am. Are you planning on going into that meeting?"

Monica glanced past the chubby lady and toward her colleagues a few feet behind her. There were six women and three men. They all looked so serious, and Monica wondered what the chaos was about. She did see some were holding signs but they were pointed toward the ground so she couldn't read them. She glanced back to the silver haired lady and nodded. "Yes, I was on my way inside."

"Ma'am, forgive me for asking, but do you have a loved one that is gay?"

"Yes, my son is. Why?"

"We," the lady gestured to her friends behind her, "want to help you. You must be devastated."

"No, not at all." There was something peculiar about the lady that Monica didn't like.

"You do realize that your son will not be allowed in God's kingdom, don't you? Your son is sinning in the worst way."

Monica glanced at a guy that was flipping a sign around for a lady going into the meeting to read. She silently read the ugly words: ***God hates Faggots. Save your child while you still can.*** Monica glared at the lady. "Are you kidding me? You came to preach to me about something that you know nothing about?" Monica had just come face to face with some real-live *haters,* and it infuriated her. She couldn't believe they had the nerve to show up at this private meeting to protest.

"You are not helping your son by accepting his disgusting behavior," the lady continued as if she didn't want to accept Monica's refusal for help.

"You don't know anything, lady." Monica tried to step around the lady, but the lady moved back in front of her.

"I know your son is full of sin and is going to go to Hell for it."

Monica's adrenaline increased. How dare this woman. "You better get the hell out of my way!" She shouted over the lady's shoulder at her followers, "Don't you people have something better to do? Like minding your own damn business!" Monica was furious as hell. She was so close to shoving this lady out of her way!

Thankfully, she changed her mind. She realized that could get her a one way ticket to jail and that was the last thing she needed right now. Instead she stepped around the lady. "Stay away from me," she hissed instead.

By then other people were walking into the meeting, which encouraged the protesters even more. They started waving their signs and chanting vile words about gays.

Monica hurried toward the building as the ringing of their words filled her head. She was sure her face was beat red. She rushed toward the door.

"Don't worry about them." A tall, dark haired man held the door open for her. "You have to learn to ignore them. They come around a lot. If they think they can get to you, they will keep harassing you. We just pretend we don't see them and go about our business."

As angry as Monica was, she appreciated the good-looking guy's kind words. "Thank you," she said as she glided through the door. "Wow, they made me so mad."

"You must be new?"

She smiled. "Is it that obvious?"

"Most people have a lot of anger when they first join these meetings, but as time goes on the anger disappears. And it will for you too."

"Not toward people like that it won't." Monica gestured toward the people picketing.

"I know...they are annoying." He held out his hand. "My name is Simon. Simon Cox."

"Oh, I am Monica Myers." She shook his hands. "Thanks for the advice."

"You're welcome. I have a gay son. How about you?"

"Me, too. I just found out a few weeks ago."

"I see," he said. "Then it is still fresh for you." He motioned for her to sit in the chair next to him.

"Thank you." Monica was a little rattled by the guy's charming nature. She had to remind herself that she was still married.

"My son, Tony, is twenty-eight. I have known for several years, and I am perfectly fine with it. It took me a while to accept it, and I had to do a lot of researching and soul searching before I came to the conclusion that it is okay to be gay. I didn't realize how common it was now-a-days. And more and more people are coming out."

"I guess I have a thing or two to learn yet," she said, glancing toward the entrance. "They made me furious. I just can't believe that people can be that rude."

"I know what you mean," Simon agreed.

The lady at the front of the room began talking and the crowd grew quiet.

Monica got lost in her own thoughts as the lady rattled on introductions. She'd been so close to doing something violent to that nasty woman outside that it was too hard to just brush off.

Monica had never been in a fight in her life, nor had she ever had the desire to punch anyone, but she did tonight. She didn't care how old the lady was. She would have never thought someone could provoke her, the way that woman had done.

She glanced over at Simon and was glad he'd come to her rescue and calmed her down. She knew she had a long road ahead of her because she was certain there would be many more situations like tonight. She just prayed that she had the strength to stay focused and not to let those kind of people get to her.

She again repeated the vow she'd made so many times before: *I will do everything I possibly can to keep my children safe from this evil world.*

Chapter Five

Saturday, June 14, 2008

Monica sucked in a deep breath as she glanced toward the entrance of the mall. "Are you sure you're alright with this?"

Crystal giggled. "Too late now. I'm here. Let's do this. God, I hope I don't see anyone that knows Rick." She laughed again. "He would never believe the truth, you know."

"No one we know will see us. We are over an hour away from home."

Monica grabbed Crystal's hand as they entered the mall. "Now be serious, please. No laughing!"

Crystal smiled. "Okay I will try. But no tongue and I mean it!" She tried to suppress the giggles but a small one escaped anyway.

Monica squeezed her hand as they passed an elderly couple. The couple stared as if they'd seen a ghost, which didn't surprise Monica.

Crystal's bold smile quickly faded. "Okay, I'll stop now."

"Did you see them look at us?" Monica growled.

"Well, Monica—as unfair as it is... most gays don't show affection in public malls."

"But why not? My husband has held my hand before or gave me a peck on the lips in public." She pulled Crystal toward a bench to sit. "It shouldn't be any different for homosexuals. They should be able to show affection in public, also."

"Oh, I totally agree with you. But it is just the way society is. We can't change it."

"Oh, but we can let them know they are wrong!" Monica wrapped her arm around Crystal and pulled her close to her.

A man and woman with a young boy were walking in their direction until they spotted Monica and Crystal. They quickly jerked the boy around so he didn't see them and proceeded to drag him in the opposite direction. A couple of high school girls walked by and stared. They giggled, and the tall, blond haired whispered something funny in the shorter girl's ear and they both giggled again.

Across the aisle two college-age guys waited in line for a pretzel. It didn't take long for Monica to figure out which one was the smart-ass.

He was the one with the thick glasses and a half-cocky - grin spread across his face. He nudged his friend and nodded toward Monica and Crystal. "Hey, look. I think someone needs to get a room," he said loudly enough for Monica to hear.

The last few minutes Monica had watched people judge her because of what they thought was her sexual orientation. And with every stare and every giggle, Monica grew more and more furious. She could only imagine what it must feel like to actually be gay and be treated with such disrespect. But the comment from the last guy really hit a raw nerve and Monica was quick to respond. "Maybe you need some new glasses. I wasn't making out with my girlfriend—I was simply telling her I loved her. Do you have a problem with that?"

Monica heard Crystal gasp. She didn't know who was more surprised by her outburst: Crystal or the arrogant dude. He seemed taken back and was speechless for a few seconds. Finally he shrugged. "Chill, lady. I was just kidding." He spun back around to the counter to retrieve his pretzel.

Crystal whispered, "What are you doing? Trying to get us killed? Come on, Monica, you can't let these people get to you!"

"I'm sorry! But have you noticed the way people are treating us? It's like we have some contagious disease or something! That man and woman didn't even want their boy to see us. They pulled him in another direction just to avoid us."

"Did you really think you would get a different kind of reaction here?" Crystal stood and pulled Monica to her feet. "Come on… let's go shop while we are here."

Monica's voice cracked, "It's not fair. I don't want my son to go through life being ashamed of who he is."

"Kade is not ashamed of who he is. You should know that. Look how much he's accomplished in just a few short years. I am sure he understands that some people are just not on the same page as the rest of us. They just don't get it. And the sad part is that most of them don't want to change the way they think and feel. They are still stuck in another century."

"It makes me so mad though. I feel so helpless."

"It is a motherly instinct to protect your children. So, of course, you're going to feel helpless. But you're not going to help Kade by acting out in rage toward people that don't understand him. You can't take it personally, honey." Crystal snatched a tissue out of her purse and dabbed at the tears slowly caressing the side of Monica's nose. "Kade needs you to stay calm and keep believing in him. It doesn't matter to him what other people think as much as it matters to him what *you* think."

Monica suddenly felt foolish. Everything Crystal was saying made sense. "You're my angel." She hugged her friend and then pulled away from her. "You're so smart. This was a dumb idea. You are totally right."

Crystal patted Monica on the back. "That'a girl!"

"Okay, we don't have to pretend to be gay any longer. I got a taste of what homosexuals have to go through. Even though I still don't think it is fair, I know there has to be other ways for me to reach out to people." She rested her hands on her hips. "I will try to find a way to make people understand that they need to get their head out of the ass and learn to accept others that are different!" She laughed out loud and Crystal joined in.

"Okay, maybe I need to go about it a little differently. I'll have to think some more on it." She grabbed Crystal's hand and then quickly let go. "Come on let's go check out the sales."

***

Kade wasn't surprised how his mother had been treating him. He always knew she would be more supportive than his father. His dad hadn't even talked to him since he found out, nor did it surprise him. He knew how his dad felt about gays. All the sarcastic comments he'd made over the years still haunted him.

It hurt that his father thought less of him because of his sexual orientation. But it also angered him that he wasn't more understanding like his mother.

Kade had gone the extra mile to excel in high school so his parents would be proud of him. Maybe deep down he thought if they were proud of him, they wouldn't be so disappointed when they found out about his sexuality. He should have known better with his father.

Kade gently pushed on the horn to let John know he was waiting. His father was bent over the engine of a car in the driveway. Kade sure didn't want to blare on the horn and scare Papa Logan; hard telling what he'd do. The last few times Kade had picked up John, Papa Logan had been on the porch. Kade smiled at the nickname him and John had given his father. His real name was Paul Logan—but Papa Logan seemed to fit better. Rarely did he look in Kade's direction when he came to pick up John. Usually he'd be tinkering around with something. He seldom looked up to tell John goodbye either.

John didn't like to talk much about his family life. If Kade asked something in particular about his mom or dad, John would give a short reply and then change the subject. Kade didn't want to pressure him but he had the feeling that home life wasn't too pleasant for John.

Kade was glad they'd become even better friends over the last few weeks. It was nice to find someone that could relate to him and that he could talk to. Although John still claimed he was going to pretend to be straight—Kade knew it wouldn't be easy. *You can't deny how your heart truly feels. You can't pretend you are attracted to the opposite sex if you're really not. Maybe temporarily you can, but how can anyone ever really be happy by doing that,* Kade wondered.

John pounced out of the house, carrying a garbage bag full of trash. He lifted the lid of the outside trash can next to the garage and stuffed the sack in. He yelled bye to his dad, but his dad didn't blink. He looked to be in deep thought as he studied a part he'd pulled out of the car.

"Hey, how's it going?" Kade asked as soon as John climbed into his car.

"Not bad. That's nice of your mom to have me for dinner again so soon." He slammed the door shut. "I am sorry about your parents splitting up."

Kade had told John about his parents breaking up and about believing that he was the reason for it. "Oh well, it is what it is. I can't make my dad accept who I am any more than you can make your parents accept you." He wasn't sure if he should have thrown the last comment in but it was too late now.

John's eyes widened. "It's not the same. My dad would really come unglued. And he wouldn't just leave. He would make me pay in horrible ways."

Kade didn't know quite how to respond to that statement.

"Well, I don't think anyone should be treated badly for something that they have no control over." He pushed on the gas. "But let's talk about something not so depressing-- like food. Are you hungry?"

"Starved—especially for your mom's cooking. She's the best."

"I hope you like Mexican. She's making tacos and enchiladas for dinner."

"Yum. You know I love Mexican." John's eyes narrowed "I bet you put that bug in her ear?"

"Maybe." Kade smiled. "She likes you; and she loves to cook so you lucked out."

"She has to be the sweetest lady I know. You don't know how lucky you are to have her, Kade."

"Yeah, I do. And I am thankful—for my sister too! I never thought I'd say that!" Kade laughed. "You don't have to worry about Karm. She knows all about us too. She's cool with it."

"I wish I had your family." John grew quiet as he shifted his eyes out the window.

Kade couldn't help but wonder what was going through John's head. He feared John's home life was worse than he imagined. By the looks of Papa Logan and what little he'd heard about his mother, it didn't sound like a very nurturing family.

Kade would like to help him, but until John opened up more, there wasn't much he could do. But when John was ready to talk, he would be there for him.

***

Monica pulled the enchiladas out of the oven and placed them on a hot pad on the table. She knew the boys would be home any second, and Karmen and her friend Mindy had just returned home from the local mall. The girls had spent the day shopping for swimsuits.

Monica loved to cook for Kade and Karmen and their friends. She loved it when they had company over. It filled the loneliness in her life that she'd been encountering since Wayne had left.

She also loved the fact that John was such a sweetheart. She couldn't imagine anyone not liking him—*nor judging him for being gay*, she thought suddenly. She still hadn't got over the earlier incident at the mall. The way she was treated was uncalled for.

The front screen door slammed. Monica sighed and reminded herself not to slip and make any remarks about the earlier occurrences at the mall. Kade would be furious.

She spun around just as Kade and John entered the kitchen. "Hi, boys. I hope you're hungry." She snatched the taco sauce out of the refrigerator.

"Starved, to say the least," Kade announced as he kissed his mother on the cheek.

"Yeah I haven't eaten either. I have been saving up for tonight," John added.

"Great! It's ready so let's dig in." Monica called down the hall. "Karmen, you girls come and eat."

In a matter of minutes, they were all sitting around the table feasting on the Mexican meal. The girls chatted nonstop about the latest swimsuits in style, while the boys discussed the horse rides they had recently encountered.

Monica enjoyed the conversations. And the laughter improved her mood tremendously.

It was close to 10:00 p.m. when John said he probably should be heading home. They'd spent the last four hours playing cards.

"Thank you so much Monica for having me tonight. This has been so much fun and the meal was delicious."

"You're welcome. Come back anytime, John." She walked the boys to the front door.

Kade was the first to step outside. He suddenly froze. "Omigod, I don't believe this."

Monica, puzzled, stepped outside and peered over John's shoulder. She gasped. "Holy crap! What the hell! Who would do such a thing?" she snapped. Her eyes scanned the length of the street as her rage increased. In the front lawn

61

someone had spray painted '**We don't want fags in our neighborhood**' in bold white letters.

Monica was fuming. "Who did this?" she screamed into the street.

Kade shook his head. "Mom, it's okay. I will mow it when I get home!"

"The hell you will!" Monica ran into the street and hollered, "I'm calling the police unless someone fesses up to this."

"Mom, please don't. It's okay. I have thick skin."

John bowed his head. "I shouldn't have come tonight."

"What?" Monica turned toward the boys. Her heart ached for them. How could anyone be this cruel! "What do you mean? Don't you dare stay away because of this! Do you understand me, John?"

"Okay, Monica. Thanks."

"Please, Mom, don't do anything stupid. Please don't call the police and make a big scene." Kade wrapped his arm around his mother's shoulders. "Can't we just forget it?"

As much as Monica wanted to pursue the evil act, she could tell how much it meant to Kade not to. "Okay, I won't. Go ahead and take John home."

"Thanks, Mom. You're the best." He kissed her on the cheek before jumping in his car. He rolled down the window as he was backing out. "I will mow as soon as I get back. I'm sorry, Mom."

"What the heck for?" she called out. "You didn't do anything! It is these idiot neighbors we have." She didn't care who heard her! She couldn't believe people could be so callous. The car was already down the street but Monica still was upset. "Stupid neighbors—we are not leaving!

You hear me? We are not leaving," she screamed into the silent night.

Karmen and Mindy had come outside to see what the commotion was.

"Did you see who did this?" Karmen's mouth hung open as she stared at the words. "Poor Kade and John. This is so wrong, Mom."

She hated even Karmen and Mindy to see the ugly words. "Go back inside and flip on the outside lights. I am going to mow it right now!" Monica marched to the shed and spun the combination lock. "And I hope I wake everyone up in this damn neighborhood. I dare anyone to step outside and ask me what I am doing mowing so late. So help me, I will let you know exactly how I feel." She jerked the lawn mower out of the shed as Karmen ran back inside to flip the lights on.

"You want me to do it, Mom?" Karmen asked.

"Thanks, but I want to do it. I will be in shortly." She fired the lawn mower up and glanced up and down the street, daring anyone to walk outside and challenge her. She was ready for them.

Tears streamed down her cheeks as she pushed the lawn mower over the white paint. She wasn't going to let anyone treat her son like he was a monster.

She was determined to find out who caused Kade and John to look so devastated tonight! *This isn't funny at all,* she thought. It was the cruelest thing she'd ever witness. She couldn't believe anyone could be so insensitive. She wanted everyone to know what a horrible joke this was and how wrong it was for her son or anyone else, for that matter, to be treated with such malice.

She had so much to say but first she had to get someone to listen! And that is exactly what she planned on doing.

She was going so support the gays by trying to educate those that didn't understand. "I'll find a way to be heard. If they want to close their ears, I will pry them open!" she growled.

Chapter Six

Monday, June 16, 2008

Monica glanced at the clock on the computer. It was almost midnight. She had been off and on the computer all day. She was sure she'd researched every gay organization there was.

She was still upset about the unpleasant incident on Saturday night. It angered her even more that she had no clue who did it. Every time she drove by any of the neighbors she'd catch herself staring and wondering if it could have been them—and if they caught her staring, she'd quickly look away. She'd always offered a friendly wave in the past—but not anymore. She couldn't bring herself to be congenial without knowing who the backstabber actually was.

Kade hadn't said a word about that night. He'd come home after taking John home and gone straight to bed.

Sunday he'd snuck off to work before Monica ever got out of bed. She knew he had the early shift but he'd usually wake her and let her know he was leaving.

She was sure it was still bothering him. If only she could make all his pain go away. She'd do anything not to see her son hurting. She didn't even know the right words to console him anymore.

She was certain if more people were educated on homosexuality, they wouldn't be so fast to judge them. The local organizations weren't enough anymore because they weren't reaching as many people as they needed to be.

Her first thought was the schools. *Why wasn't homosexuality being taught in psychology or sociology classes?* She'd read one in ten males were gay; so why was it not being taught in education? She didn't understand that. If more teenagers were taught in schools that it wasn't abnormal to be gay, maybe they wouldn't be harassed as much. Homosexuals need to be accepted in school and the students need to be taught not to bully them! She was certain the best way to do this was to create a more diverse array of topics in school; ones that affect all students—not just the majority.

Her mind had been racing all day. She wasn't quite sure where to start so she typed a letter up explaining the situation and made copies. She planned to send the copies out to multiple places.

Monica yawned. She hadn't slept much the last couple of nights and was suddenly feeling fatigue. She decided to call it a night and start fresh first thing in the morning. She turned the computer off and flipped off the light switch.

It was extremely quiet as she made her way to her bedroom. Kade and Karmen had gone to bed over an hour ago.

She pulled back the covers and climbed into her warm bed. It was the nights that were lonely. It was only then that she would allow herself to think of Wayne. She wondered if he was sleeping well without her, and sometimes she wondered if he was even sleeping alone.

She'd talked to him a few days ago and knew he'd already filed the paperwork for the divorce. She had cried briefly but the reality was she'd seen it coming and wasn't too surprise about any of it. She had wondered for awhile what went wrong between them but then realized nothing went wrong—they were just never right for each other in the first place. It was like two totally different people with different views trying to make it work.

Even if Kade wasn't gay, something else would have come up. Monica realized now that their marriage was doomed to fail sooner or later.

It was hard at first but each day it grew easier and easier. She knew she was right for defending Kade and she pitied Wayne for missing out on his son's life because of his foolish views on homosexuality. One day he would realize he was wrong, but it may be too late by then.

Monica flipped over on her side and pulled the covers up under her chin. She didn't want to waste any more time thinking about Wayne. She closed her eyes and in a matter of minutes, she'd floated off to dreamland.

***

Tuesday, July 1, 2008

Monica spun around and examined all angles of the image in the mirror. The tailored suit gave her a professional look; just the way she wanted to present herself. It had been two weeks since Monica mailed her letters to everyone that she could think of that would be associated with the school boards.

Finally, on Thursday, she'd received a response, suggesting she attend the next upcoming board meeting to discuss her concerned topic. She checked her watch just as the doorbell rang. She peeked around the curtain to see Simon's car. She had agreed to let him take her to the meeting for moral support. They'd gone out for coffee a couple times after the PFLAG meetings, and Monica had explained to him what she was trying to accomplish. Simon had praised her efforts and encouraged her to follow through with it. It had been just the kind of push she needed. Although Kade and Karmen supported what she was trying to do, they weren't quite sure which direction she should go, whereas Simon had many helpful suggestions and was very knowledgeable on the past and progress of the homosexual community.

She snatched her purse off the dresser and hurried toward the front of the house.

She pulled the front door open and her insides tingled at the sight of him. "Hi. I'm impressed—you're right on time," she teased. She was glad she'd decided against waiting until her divorce was final to date him. It was only a matter of time after all.

"Why, of course. Were you expecting anything different?" Simon smiled. "You are ready, right?" he taunted back as he glanced as his watch.

"You bet." She grabbed the briefcase next to the door and followed Simon out to the car.

As they drove to the meeting Simon quizzed her on questions that she might be asked. She tried to respond without stumbling over her words but a couple of times she had to refer to her notes.

Simon pulled into an empty space as he glanced down at his watch. "We are a few minutes early." He turned off the car and turned toward Monica. "I know you are nervous but you will do fine. I am proud of what you are doing. You know this could be huge if you can make them listen to you."

Monica swallowed—his words were sincere and tugged at her heart. *What a good man,* she thought. "Thank you and thank you for coming with me."

"No—thank you for letting me." He jumped out and hurried to open the door for her.

She climbed out and took a deep breath as she grabbed her briefcase. "I'm ready. Let's do this."

Simon reached for the briefcase to carry. Monica was stunned. It had been so long since a man had offered such a courteous gesture.

She remained silent until they were inside and seated at a table. She retrieved her folder with her paperwork in it as the room slowly filled.

After several minutes, all of the seats were occupied. A tall, elderly gentleman with a receding hairline and wireframe glasses stood to welcome everyone. He introduced himself as Stuart Grisley, President of the School Board.

He reminded Monica of Mr. Piper, a stern math teacher she'd had in 8th grade. His voice was loud and serious and every once a while he would try to add a joke. She didn't dislike his attitude but she wasn't quite sure if she was going to like him, either.

She had to sit through all of the old business before her topic was addressed. Simon squeezed her hand as her name was called.

She quickly introduced herself and Simon. She went on to add the years she'd been teaching. She briefly talked about Kade and Karmen. After bragging about Kade's academic achievement and his involvement in his class, she ended by stating that her son was gay. She went on with all the statics she'd learned about gays and informed the board that one out of every ten males are gay.

She described the problem about how gays are ridiculed and bullied throughout the schools, and how it is time for us to intervene and do something about it. She explained that she thought homosexuals were being treated so badly because the students weren't educated enough about homosexuals in our society.

She explained how she believed that teaching homosexuality in certain courses could help bridge the gap. She agreed that it was hard to believe in something that society hadn't been educated about, and she'd been just as guilty herself. She continued to give details on how beneficial it could be if the schools had the proper education. Monica preached how homosexuality could go from a ridiculed minority group to students that didn't feel ashamed of who they were. And if these students felt accepted, the suicide rate would go down.

Monica glanced around the room. "It is so important for schools to stress that homosexuality is natural and shouldn't be looked down upon. Maybe then students would start accepting homosexuals more and less bullying would take place."

Monica talked a good twenty minutes, introducing the problems and then suggesting solutions. She finally closed her speech and asked if there were any questions she could answer.

A lady with dark hair, who was trying to wear a trendy suit that was too tight for her, stood. "Mrs. Myers?"

"Please call me Monica." She guessed the lady to be in her mid forties.

"Hi. My name is Laurie. No offense, Monica—but if we do that, wouldn't we be encouraging homosexuality to the students?"

Monica asked puzzled, "I'm not quite sure I follow your question?"

Another middle-aged guy spoke out loudly, "Because it is a choice that the students make!" His tone grew louder. "For crying out loud, don't you read the bible? It says so right in there."

Laurie spoke again, "That was the point I was trying to make too."

Monica bit her lower lip as she tried to stay calm. "Oh, but that is not true. My son and my family are very religious."

Stuart quickly interrupted, "Listen up! Religious is not the issue here and will not be discussed in this meeting." He nodded to the girl scribbling down notes. "Scratch anything that was said involving religion input." He glanced around the room. "Are there any other questions for Mrs. Myers?"-

A plump, silver-haired lady raised her hand.

Stuart pointed to the lady. "Yes, Silvia?"

"I am afraid I will have to vote against this proposal." She glanced toward Monica. "I mean, I feel for your son and the others out there. But is it really fair for the students that aren't gay to sit through a class that involves customs, thoughts, and sex with same sex couples?" She snarled her nose. "I mean, really? I know I wouldn't want *my* kids to sit through it."

Monica was quick to respond. "What about my child that has to sit through sex education for heterosexuals? That is not fair for my child either. And aren't we supposed to be teaching our children that we should all be treated as equals?"

Another lady interrupted, "I think what Silvia is trying to say is that it could be traumatic toward some kids that don't understand the homosexual lifestyle."

Monica's nose flared as her rage increased. "My point exactly! That's why we need to educate students more on the topic." She inhaled a deep breath. "Homosexuals have been around for a long time. In the past they have had to be very discreet about it because society didn't accept it. Now more people are coming out of the closet because people are becoming more educated on it. They are realizing now that it is a genetic issue and that is why homosexuals will always be around. And if we don't start educating our children on it, the bullying will never stop. I don't think anyone should go through school being ashamed of who they are!"

A petite lady in the back of the room spoke up. "Nice to meet you, Monica. My name is Joan." She hesitated as she glanced around the room. She finally spoke in a soft voice, "I praise you for what you are trying to do, Monica." She kept her eyes on Monica as if she was scared to let her eyes wander too far to the left or right. "I had a lesbian sister that was taunted so badly in high school..." She paused to retrieve a tissue out of her purse. "She overdosed purposely when she was only nineteen years old." Joan dabbed at her nose with the Kleenex. "I wish they would have had something like this back when she was in school and maybe...just maybe... she would still be alive."

The room grew quite as Joan's story sunk in.

Monica shook her head, "Joan, I am so sorry for your loss. Thank you for sharing that story with us."

Joan glanced around the room. "I have never shared that story with anyone. And I couldn't find a better time to share it than now." She glanced back at Monica. "You will have my vote."

"Thank you," Monica said.

Stuart stood, obviously, untouched by Joan's story. "I think we need to wrap this up. Does anyone else have anything else to add?"

Simon raised his hand and Stuart nodded toward him.

"I also have a gay son. I was like most people and didn't know anything about the homosexual lifestyle until it happened to my family. A lot of parents don't want to accept that *their* child could be gay. So they close their eyes to it instead of embracing them and trying to help them feel comfortable in their own skin. We, as parents, need to protect our kids, and we shouldn't let their sexuality preference interfere with the way we feel about them." Simon nodded to Monica. "Monica has brought up a lot of good points, and I hope each of you will think about what she's said when you cast your vote. Thank you"

Monica stood and shook hands with Stuart. "Thank you for allowing me to talk today." She gathered her papers and stuck them in her briefcase.

The room applauded as Simon picked up her briefcase. She turned and waved before following Simon out of the room.

"That was tough," she said as soon as she was outside.

"You did great!" Simon spun her toward him and rubbed her shoulders.

She sighed, "I think most of them hated me."

Suddenly Simon bent forward and kissed her on the lips. He quickly pulled back. "I'm sorry." He blushed. "That was probably inappropriate; I am just so proud of you."

Although Monica didn't mind the kiss, it did leave her speechless for a second. She had a warm fuzzy feeling from knowing that he approved of what she was doing. It felt great knowing he was on her side when so many were against her. "No, it's okay." She grabbed his hand as they walked to the car. "I am so glad you came with me and supported me."

Simon unlocked Monica's door and opened it for her. "I think you stood your ground well."

"I think having you next to me gave me the strength I needed to speak my true feelings. I don't know if I would have done as well had I been alone." She stared out the window as Simon drove. "But I still don't think they bought what I had to say."

"Just give them time to let it all sink in and discuss what you had to say. This is all new to them. It might take awhile for them to understand the overall picture. Just remember that some people are stuck in their own beliefs—they refuse to have an open mind."

"I'm scared they are going to say no, Simon." Monica's eyes turned watery. "They *have* to pass this. There have to be some changes made in the schools!"

"I hope they do pass it too—but if not, don't give up." He pulled up in front of Monica's house and turned the car off. He then leaned across the seat and gave Monica a more passionate kiss. "That time was because I couldn't resist."

She giggled like a school girl. Monica had liked the kiss just as much as she enjoyed his company. "I would invite you in, but the kids will be coming home soon. And I don't know if…."

Simon quickly interrupted. "On no, I wouldn't do that. I need to get home and do some laundry anyway." He opened his door, "But I will walk you to your door."

"Thanks but that's not necessary. I do appreciate the offer though." She didn't wait for him to argue back. She immediately reached over and kissed him on the cheek. "Thanks again."

She jumped out of the car and hurried up the sidewalk. She waved one last time before going through the door.

Monica flopped down in the recliner, enjoying the juvenile sensation in her stomach. She felt like a young school girl again with a crush on a good-looking senior. She hadn't been this happy for a long time. If only this feeling could last forever.

Chapter Seven

Thursday, July 3, 2008

Kade slid into the booth across from John. He finally talked John into letting him treat him to dinner. It hadn't been easy, either. John hadn't wanted to do much of anything the last couple of weeks. It seemed like ever since the yard incident, John had tried to keep his distance from Kade. They still texted back and forth but John didn't seem to want to hang out anymore. And Kade didn't quite understand why.

Kade waited until they had placed their order and then he spoke, "Is everything okay?"

John glanced around the restaurant. "Sure. Why?"

"You have just seemed distant lately. And I haven't been able to get you to go anywhere." Kade paused. "I thought you enjoyed horseback riding."

"I do. I just have been busy."

Kade remained silent. He thought John would offer more information but instead he fiddled with the dessert and drink menus.

"John, is everything okay at home?"

"Yeah. Why?" He glanced up as the waitress set down their burgers and fries.

Kade thanked the waitress and waited for her to leave before continuing, "I just feel like you are not telling me something. I am your friend, you know?" He waited but John remained silent as he chewed his food. "If something is troubling you, I want to help."

"Really, I'm fine." John dipped a french fry in ketchup and then stuffed it in his mouth.

Three high school boys shot through the restaurant's front door, laughing loudly.

Kade didn't miss the way John glanced their way and then quickly lowered his eyes back to his food.

The tall, slender kid instantly recognized John. "Hey, look its Fairy Johnny."

The other boys laughed which encouraged the kid to continue, "Fairy Johnny, is that your new beau with you?" The other two boys shrieked with laughter.

Kade was getting angrier by the second. "You know those guys?"

A young brunette girl immediately approached the boys to seat them.

Kade's voice grew louder, "They say one more word and I'm going to give them a piece of my mind. The jackasses."

John's head shot up. "No! Don't, please. Just ignore them. Please don't say anything, Kade."

Kade shook his head. "But that is uncalled for, John. You don't need to take crap like that."

"I do all the time. It is no big deal." John gestured to his body. "Look at me. What can I do about it? Beat them up? They would pounce on me in a second if I ever got mouthy with them."

Kade knew John had a good point. John was a petite guy and didn't look like he had a muscle in his body.

On one hand Kade didn't think he could whip any of their butts either but he would take a beating before he'd let them call him names. He imagined that was just the difference between John and himself.

Suddenly, Kade had a change of thought. No one had ever insinuated that he was gay. He'd always been able to keep it a secret. Whereas with John, it's pretty obvious that he is gay. Kade figured he was probably taunted a lot about it too. He figured if he were in John's shoes, he too, would learn to ignore the accusations.

"I'm sorry, John. I won't say anything."

Within minutes, the three boys had forgotten about them and were laughing about something else while they studied the menu.

"It's okay." John wiped his mouth with the napkin and tossed it on his plate. "I'm ready to get out of here."

"Yeah, me too." Kade quickly paid the waitress and they hurried to the car.

After driving in silence for awhile, Kade finally spoke. "You feel like going horseback riding? We still got a couple hours of sunlight left."

"Thanks, Kade, but I'm really not in the mood. Maybe another time."

"Okay. You want to go anywhere else?"

"No, I need to get home before my dad gets home. Thanks for taking me to dinner. Maybe I can do the same for you sometime?"

"No problem."

They rode the rest of the way to John's house in silence.

Kade pulled up to the curb just as Papa Logan was climbing out of his car. "Sorry, it looks like he beat us."

John's face paled. "Oh, God, this is bad, Kade."

Kade was baffled, "What do you mean?"

"Oh my, this is so bad. He is going to kill me." His eyes watered as his father's eyes traveled to Kade's vehicle. "He knows that you are gay." John hesitated, not wanting to get out. "I'm not supposed to be hanging out with you anymore."

"That's crazy! How did he find that out?" Kade asked.

"He found that Advocate magazine you gave me. I couldn't let him think it was mine. I'm sorry, Kade."

"It's okay, but...." He couldn't finish because Papa Logan was marching toward the car with a look of hate written on all over his face. "Don't get out, John."

"I have to. Oh, shit!"

"Don't get out, John! Stay at my house tonight."

Too late—John had already opened the door.

Papa Logan immediately grabbed John by the arm and jerked him out of the car. "Get your ass out of that car!" He leaned down and glared at Kade. "You get your queer ass off my property and don't ever come back here again." He slammed the door and shoved John toward the house.

Kade's whole body was trembling. He'd never been so scared for someone like he was John right now. He suddenly jumped out of the car and screamed toward John, "Don't worry, John. I'm calling the police."

Papa Logan spun around. "You mind your own fucking business, smart ass fag."

John glanced over his shoulder and mumbled loudly. "Don't Kade. Please!"

Papa Logan pushed John through the front door and slammed it shut. Kade just stood there, staring up at the house.

He jumped back in the car and sped away. His mind raced. He could *call* the police but what would he tell them. He actually couldn't say he saw Papa Logan do anything violent except shove John. But he could explain to them John's past experience with his father. And let them know that the man had abused John in the past.

He snatched his phone and started to dial 911 but as soon as he got the first one dialed, he had second thoughts and quickly disconnected. John's words echoed in his head, *'Don't Kade. Please.'*

What if he made life worse for John by calling the police? "Oh, God, what do I do?" he mumbled out loud. He tried fighting back the tears but it was no use. The tears surfaced and spilled down his cheeks. He had never been so torn and indecisive before. He felt so useless!

***

Monica stared at the TV. She had no clue how long she'd been sitting there. She didn't even have a clue what show she was watching. All she could think about was the recent phone call from Stuart. They had voted against her proposal.

Monica was so depressed. She'd been afraid they would say no. Stuart tried to explain all the different channels it would have to go through before it was approved. And that they would have to have an open meeting for the public eventually.

She tried arguing with him but didn't get anywhere.

Her cell phone rang. She figured it was Simon. She'd left him a message earlier, letting him know it didn't pass.

"Hello."

"Oh, Monica," Simon said, "I am so sorry."

"Thanks. Yeah, me too. I'm pretty down in the dumps right now."

"You want me to come over?"

"I appreciate the offer, but I think just need some time alone," she said.

"You know I don't mind. I hate you being by yourself."

"It's okay. I'll be fine. The kids will be coming home before long anyway." She stood, slowly paced across the room, and stared out the window. "They will be disappointed too."

"Well, don't give up. We will just take the next step," he said.

"Which is?"

"I don't know. We will have to do some research."

"Thanks, Simon, for everything." She saw Kade pull into the driveway. "Hey, can I talk to you later. Kade' s home."

"Sure. Give me a call if you need me."

"I will. Thanks." She tossed the cell phone on the couch and hurried to open the door for Kade.

The moment she saw Kade she knew something was wrong. She seldom witnessed him crying but could tell that he had been. "Kade, you okay?"

"Not really, Mom." He dropped down to the recliner. "I don't know what to do. I think John is in a lot of trouble." He quickly explained the incident with Papa Logan. "I don't know if I should call the police or not, especially since John asked me not to."

"Wow, that's a tough one," Monica said. "Poor John." She ventured to the couch. "And I thought I was having a bad day."

"Oh no, Mom. Did you get news from the board?"

Her bad news seemed petty now after hearing what Kade and John had gone through. "Yeah, I did. It didn't pass. But I'm not giving up that easily."

"I'm sorry, mom." Kade flicked away a tear that had escaped down his cheek. "I guess this world just doesn't have room for my kind." He stood. "It's not fair, and I don't even understand."

Monica let the tears slide down her own cheeks. "I know, honey. And I am so sorry."

He kissed his mother on the cheek. "You're the best mom ever. I am so glad I got you." He turned down the hallway. "I'm going to my room and try calling John."

"Okay, sweetie. I don't know what to tell you to do. I guess just keep trying to get a hold of John and make sure he is okay."

"Okay. I'll be in my room if you need me." Kade hurried down the hall into his room.

Monica dropped back down on the couch and stared at the TV. She didn't understand why life had to be so difficult.

***

Later: 10:30 p.m.

Kade took his shower and settled in his bed to watch a sitcom. He was relieved that he'd finally received a text earlier from John. Although John hadn't disclosed any information on the situation at home, he did respond back by saying everything was okay.

Kade was glad he hadn't called the police after all. He might have made the incident a lot worse.

He'd just gotten comfortable when he got another text. Kade's heart raced as he read John's words:

Kade, thank you for being the best friend I have ever had. Thank your mom for me too. I am sorry that this will be the last text I send you. Please don't blame yourself for what I am about to do. There is nothing you could have done differently to change my mind. I have been thinking about this for a few weeks now. Now that my dad knows the truth about me, there is no use to go on any longer. The bruises he put all over me didn't even hurt as much as the words he said to me. I can live with physical pain but I can't live with a broken heart and knowing I will never make my dad happy. He's right. I am a loser and I was a mistake. I should have never been born.
Bye Kade and thank you.

Kade stared helplessly at his cell phone, trying to soak in what John was implying. His mind went numb. He couldn't believe this was happening and now he wished he would have called the police.

He jumped out of bed and threw his clothes on. He dialed John's cell as he slipped on his shoes. It went to his voice mail. "John, its Kade. Please listen to me. Please don't do anything stupid. I'm on my way there to pick you up. You can stay at my house for as long as you need to." He grabbed his keys off his dresser and ran toward the front of the house. Kade continued, "You're not a loser, John. You are the only best friend I have ever had. I would be so lost without you. Your dad is wrong. Being gay is not a shameful thing, John. Please call me. We need to talk. I'm on my way!" Kade hung up and yelled at his mom in the kitchen as he ran out the front door. "I'll be back, Mom. John is going to try to kill himself."

Chapter Eight

Kade had never been so upset. He was so worried about his friend. He repeatedly dialed John's number but it just kept going to his voice mail.

He pushed down on the gas pedal as he glanced in the rearview mirror. He couldn't help but speed. He just prayed he could get there in time before John did anything foolish.

Fifteen minutes later, Kade pulled down John's street and instantly knew he was too late. He could see the siren lights as he neared. Sure enough, as he approached John's, he spotted the ambulance parked right in front of his house. A group of bystanders stood in a circle, waiting to see what the chaos was about.

John parked his car and jumped out. He ran toward the front door just as a policeman stopped him.

"You can't go in there," the policeman shouted at Kade.

"But it is my best friend. I need to talk to him."

"I'm sorry, but you will have to wait out here."

Just then Papa Logan held the screen door open as they carried a stretcher out.

Kade knew immediately of the outcome. The attendants didn't seem to be in a big hurry like they would have been if they were trying to save someone. And there was a white sheet pulled over the body which he had no doubt that it was John.

The sheet over the head was turning red and Kade imagined it was from a head wound. He ventured back to the group of people who were gasping as they carried the body out and slid it into the back of the ambulance.

Kade asked, "Does anyone know what happened?"

A large frame man, who was almost as wide as he was tall spoke up, "We heard Paul Logan's son shot himself in the head." The guy shook his head. "Just killed himself for no reason." He lowered his voice, "I heard Paul was pretty nasty with the kid." He nudged a chucky woman standing next to him. "Hazel said she could hear him yelling at him from inside her house."

"Oh yeah, he was just a ranting and raving," she said quickly. "I couldn't understand what he was yelling about, though, but he sure was calling him a lot of names." She glanced toward Paul Logan talking to the policeman. "Look at him. There's not a tear in his eyes." She shook her head. "No remorse whatsoever. What the heck was he thinking?"

Kade assumed Hazel was the kind that liked chaos and gossip. And he wasn't about to offer her any more information. "Thank you," he said with a choked whisper.

He walked away from the crowd that had gathered toward his own car.

Suddenly, he heard Paul Logan's voice, "That's him, there."

Kade spun around as Paul shook his finger toward him. "That's him. He is the one that made my son gay." He shook his fist at Kade. "See what you did? This is your fault! You're to blame for my son's death!"

Kade kept walking as he heard a woman squeal and swear under her breath. He could have sworn it was Hazel.

He glanced over his shoulder and witnessed a policeman trying to calm Paul down while another policeman was walking toward Kade.

"I apologize for Mr. Logan's' rude words. I'm sure he is just upset about his son." He held out his hand. "I'm Officer Chadwick."

Kade noticed the young officer was clean-cut, from his neatly ironed shirt to his shiny polished boots. His face was cleanly shaven and the recent crew cut confirmed that he took his job serious. "I'm Kade Myers. I was a friend of John's."

"Would you mind stopping down at the station just so we can ask you a few questions about John and try to determine why he did this."

"I know why he did this," Kade said, glancing toward Paul. "His father is a jerk," he spat out. He had never hated anyone as much as he hated Paul Logan right now.

"I'm so sorry about the loss of your friend." Officer Chadwick glanced around at the crowd still gathered. "This isn't the place to talk." He handed him his card. "You mind meeting me there." He pointed to the address on the card.

"Sure, I'll be there shortly." He jumped in his car and fired it up. He couldn't wait to tell the police about Paul Logan and how he was to blame for his son's death. He wasn't going to hold back anything. Kade was going to make everyone see that papa Logan's hatred toward gays was the reason John took his own life. He couldn't even love his own son because of it.

Kade briefly thought of his own father. At least his father just ignored him and didn't voice his opinion to him. And his father would never blacken his eye no matter how much he didn't agree with Kade.

Kade still couldn't believe John was dead. Just like that—he was gone. His best friend and the only gay friend he had ever had. He couldn't control his tears any longer. They poured down his cheeks like the waterfall that John loved down by the creek. "Why, John? Why?" He hit the steering wheel with his fist. "Why didn't you let me help you? Damn it, John! You didn't have to do this!" The sobs came rapidly. "My mom loved you too. We could have helped you." He looked toward the sky, wondering if John could actually hear his words.

He wiped at his nose as he pulled up to the police station. He mumbled. "Yes, Papa Logan, I am going to make you regret the way you treated your son if it is the last thing I ever do!"

***

It had been a couple of hours since Kade had stormed out the door to go help John. Monica was worried sick. She'd tried a couple of times to call Kade's cell phone, but it kept going to his voice mail.

She walked over to the window and stared out into the gloomy night. It was after midnight so the streets were deserted. There wasn't a car in sight.

She paced back and forth in front of the window, wishing she knew John's address. If she knew the address, she could drive over there herself.

Suddenly Monica jumped at the sound of the cell phone. Although she'd heard the ringtone many of times, it still caught her off guard.

She snatched the phone off the end table, recognizing Kade's number. "Hello—Kade?"

"Yeah, Mom."

"You okay?" Her words were rushed, "You don't sound too good."

"Sorry I haven't had a chance to call you back. I have been at the police station the last couple of hours."

"What happened?" She could tell by Kade's voice that it wasn't good news.

"I didn't make it in time." Kade paused. "John killed himself. Shot himself in the head with his father's gun," he said quietly.

"Oh my God. That is horrible. But why?"

"His father found out he was gay and was giving him a rough time."

"You're kidding me! Really?" Monica was dumbfounded. "Was his father really that bad?" She grabbed a wine glass down off the top shelf. "I mean your father didn't accept you, but you would never do something like that." She poured the wine in the glass. "Would you?"

"Of course not. But his father was a lot worse that Dad. I will have to tell you about it when I get home."

"Okay, honey. I am so sorry. He was such a sweet kid. That just breaks my heart." She shook her head as the tears surfaced. "Be careful and I will see you shortly."

Monica waited until she heard the click from Kade before she allowed the tears to spill. She had wanted to be strong for Kade, but deep down her heart was breaking for this young boy that just wanted to be accepted for who he was. She couldn't believe that people could be so cruel, especially his own father.

She couldn't help but wonder how many other kids had done the same thing for the same reasons. She thought of all the kids that go through life not ever telling anyone their secret. She did the math in her head as goosebumps on the back of her neck surfaced. If the statistics were correct, Kade's school of nearly 500 students would mean that 50 of them were gay. And to her knowledge not one of them was willing to admit it. "Damn it!" She cursed under her breath, not wanting to wake up Karmen. "It's just not fair!"

Monica hurried into the computer room to boot up the computer.

She researched suicides and was shocked at all of the young suicides that were committed due to bullying. She read that in 2007 there were roughly 4000 suicide by those ranging in the teens-to-college age. It said that, although the exact figure is disputed, a good estimate is three to four percent of the suicides were committed by homosexuals, which would mean around 150 gay young people kill themselves in a year.

Monica stared at the computer screen. She couldn't believe it. She briefly thought of her own son and how his own father had disowned him. The thought of Kade taking his own life because of his dad's ignorance made her cringe. She would be devastated if he killed himself but even more so if it was because of the way he was treated.

She glanced toward the ceiling, "God, please guide me in the right direction to help these kids that can't change the way they are. Please help me to make changes in our school system so gay students aren't shunned for being different." The tears slid down her cheeks. Her mind was made up. She was going back to the school board and she was going to share John's story with them. She was going to make them see how important it was that changes be made. And she wouldn't take no for an answer this time!

Kade drove home silently. Losing John was far worse than losing his own father. He could understand why John felt the way he did. He, too, had been upset when his father had disowned him. He'd been crushed. And he'd be lying to himself if he said suicide had never crossed his mind. Actually, it had a few times earlier in his life.

Kade hadn't wanted to be gay any more than the next person. He precisely remembered the first year of high school and how he had hated it. He hated trying to fit in and having to cover up his identity. He remembered lying in bed one night and considering killing himself—that way no one would ever find out that he was gay. But the thought of his poor mom wondering where she'd gone wrong convinced him otherwise. Plus he truly believed that God had plans for him. He just wasn't sure what it was yet.

So instead he strived to be the best he could be and make his parents proud. He thought maybe they wouldn't be so disappointed when the truth did come out.

He was glad his mother knew now. Knowing that she believed in him, regardless of his sexual preference encouraged him to be proud of who he was. And her most recent words would always stay with him. "Kade, sweetie," she had said with such tenderness. "God is not cruel. He would not make you gay and then punish you if you act upon it. God is good. And the people that say God is going to punish you by sending you to Hell," she had paused and rubbed his back in the loving way that she always done. "Well, they just don't know the same God that you and I know. And we should be praying for them!" She had smiled and gave him a big hug. Kade would remember her words for as long as he lived. He had thanked God over and over that evening for giving him such an understanding mother.

He pulled up in his driveway and grabbed a tissue out of the glove compartment. He blew his nose and checked his swollen eyes. He hated for anyone to see him this upset even his own mother. *Even gay men didn't like to cry in front of people,* he thought.

He knew it was going to be a long night and he was thankful that he could share his grief with his mom. She always knew just the right things to say to ease the pain.

He climbed out of the car and glanced one last time at the sky. He mumbled under his breath, "I'm sorry, John. I wish I could have been a better friend for you." The tears surfaced again as he ran into his mother's welcoming arms.

Chapter Nine

Monday, July 7, 2008, 8:55a.m.

Monica dialed Stuart's home phone number for the fifth time. She knew it was early, but she desperately needed to talk to him. She only had a few hours of sleep the last few nights. She'd never seen her son so devastated before. It was breaking her heart.

Finally, after fourth ring, she heard his voice on the other end. "Hello."

"Mr. Grisley, this is Monica Myers."

"Oh! Hello, Monica. Please call me Stuart."

"Okay, Stuart. I apologize for calling you so early."

"Not a problem. I just finished my breakfast and was going to head down to the office."

"I really need to talk to you. Something awful has happened to a friend of my son's this weekend. He shot himself in the head. It was all because he was gay and his father wouldn't accept him."

"Oh, I am so sorry to hear that." Stuart said nonchalantly. "And I am sorry your proposal was voted against. There's not much more I can do at this time though."

Monica didn't hear any empathy in his voice like she assumed she would. His apology didn't even sound sincere. "But I need another shot. Please let me address the board members one more time. This is so important. Innocent gay students are out killing themselves because of all the discrimination." She groaned impatiently. "Please Mr. Grisley. The bullying in the school needs to be addressed immediately."

"Monica, believe me, I am aware that there is a problem. But unless we get the votes, there is nothing more I can do." He sighed impatiently. "I hate to cut this short, but I really need to be going."

"That's bologna!" Monica yelled into the phone. "Let me tell you what, *Stuart*. If you don't give me another chance to talk to the board, I will find a way to go above you and get help somewhere else. *And* I will inform everyone on how you ignored the situation."

"Are you threatening me, Monica?"

"Of course not! I'm simply stating the facts."

Stuart grew quiet and Monica wondered if he was reconsidering her offer.

"Okay, Monica. I know you are upset about your son's friend. And as much as I think this is a waste of yours and my time, I will let you have one more shot—Wednesday night at six, same place."

"Thank you. I will be there. Goodbye, Mr. Grisley." She hung up the phone.

She was so furious over his attitude that she could hardly see straight. She couldn't help but wonder if he had influenced the board members to vote against her proposal. He just didn't seem too concerned about the problem.

She spent the next few hours going over her notes and drinking a pot of coffee.

A few minutes after noon, Monica gave Simon a call and filled him in on the latest happenings. She could instantly hear the sadness in his voice when she told him about John. Unlike Stuart, the news had a different effect on Simon. She wasn't sure if it was because Simon had a gay son and could relate easier or because he was a more compassionate person that Stuart Grisley. She imagined it was a little bit of both.

"That is just horrible," Simon said. "I am so proud of you, Monica, for standing up to Mr. Grisley. He is really starting to irritate me!"

"In that case you won't mind going with me again Wednesday night, right?"

"Of course I will go. But I was really hoping to see you before then. Any chance you can get away for dinner?"

Monica's stomach churned. She was really starting to like this guy. She knew she should wait until the divorce was final just in case Wayne decided to be ornery. But she just couldn't say no. "That would be great. I could use a break from all of this."

"Okay, I will pick you up about six. See you then, Monica."

"Bye, Simon."

***

Later:

Kade tied Maggie Mae up to the tree and made his way through the tall grass to the spot that he and John last hung out. He could recall almost every conversation him and John had had the last few weeks. He kept thinking he might remember some small detail that could have been a warning sign of John's intention.

Kade picked up a rock and tossed it into the creek. He'd never felt so alone as he did now. He had tons of friends but none of them that could relate to life the same way John had. He'd shared a bond with John because they were both gay and considered outcasts.

Kade had felt comfortable around John and could confide his darkest secrets to him. Now he had no one except his mom. Although he knew she accepted him, it wasn't the same as knowing someone that was just like yourself. The only difference was that Kade believed in himself, and John hadn't value his own life.

Tears welded up behind Kade's eyelids. He'd been fighting them all day at work. Now he could finally let his guard down. "John, I don't get it," he mumbled. He glanced toward the sky. "Why couldn't you just talk to me? I would have found help for you." Kade dropped to his knees and sobbed like he'd never cried before. He had never lost a friend of any kind—not even an acquaintance in school. He never knew something could hurt so much, especially since it probably could have been prevented. If only John's father wasn't such a jack ass like all of the other haters out there! "You bastard," he screamed into the thin air. He knew no one could hear him and it made him felt so much better releasing the anger.

Suddenly he felt like he had to do something for John. Something that might help others that also felt worthless.

He quickly pulled out his cell phone and called his mother. "Mom, it's me. I want to help."

"What are you talking about, Kade?"

"We have to make the school board listen. I want to talk to them myself." He suddenly had another thought. "Mom, maybe you've been approaching the subject the wrong way."

"What do you mean?" Monica asked.

"Instead of demanding sexuality for homosexuals be taught in schools, what if we took a more acceptable approach. Such as going around and talking to the schools about bullying gays. Maybe instead of taking a big leap, we need to start off with baby steps and work our way up."

"Wow, I think you are on to something." She paused. "Yes, I think I like it a lot. I will think on this and bring it up at the meeting Wednesday night."

"Wednesday night? I'm off. I want to go with you."

Monica was silent.

"Mom, did you hear me?"

"Yes, I heard," she whispered. "I'm just a little emotional right now. Are you sure you want to go?"

"Yes, I do. Why wouldn't I?"

"I am so proud of you, Kade. You were a good friend to John. Please don't beat yourself up over his death. There wasn't anything you could have done to prevent it."

Kade didn't exactly agree with his mother but didn't say so. "Okay, I won't. I'll be home soon. And we can talk about the meeting."

"Okay. I love you, Kade. Be careful."

"I will, Mom. Love you too. Bye."

He was excited about the meeting. He was going to fight for rights in honor of John. He untied Maggie and led her to the creek to drink.

He knew he had a lot of research to do before Wednesday night. The way his mother talked about the last meeting, it wasn't an easy crowd to please. He had to get his point across one way or another. He had to do it—not only for his own sanity but, for the memory of his best friend, John.

***

Monica thanked Simon for the wonderful dinner and apologized to him once again for cutting their date short. She had already explained to him that Kade would be waiting for her to go over notes for the upcoming meeting. She was so excited that Simon and Kade both would be with her this time. With both of them by her side she knew she'd have the support she needed to speak how she genuinely felt.

Simon walked Monica to the door and kissed her gently. "I always enjoy your company. I will see you tomorrow night."

"Me, too. Thanks again, Simon."

He spun and walked toward his car. As he opened his car door, he yelled back, "You will do fine. Get some rest tonight."

Monica smiled. "I wish I had your confidence. See you Wednesday!"

"Okay, see you then." He jumped in the driver's seat.

She waved to him as he pulled away from the curb.

Monica rushed inside. Kade was already filing through papers at the kitchen table.

She dropped her purse in the arm chair and hurried toward him. "Sorry I am running a little late."

"It's okay. I have been printing information off of the Internet."

She kissed his forehead. "Find anything good?"

"Some statistics and a few interesting stories that might be convincing."

"You sure you feel up to going to this meeting?"

He looked up at his mom with red, swollen eyes. "Maybe I can't bring John back, but I sure can fight for other kids that feel like they don't have a chance in this prejudice world." He shook his head. "You wouldn't believe all the stories I have come across of homosexuals being bullied."

"Yes, I am afraid I would believe it. I have been doing my own research on it. It's just so sad. I never knew that I lived in such a cruel world. I guess you just don't pay attention to what is happening around you unless it pertains to you or someone you know."

"Mom, I am so fortunate that no one in my school knew about me. If they did, I wouldn't have been popular, and I would have been bullied like all these others." He nodded toward the pages on the table.

"I'm sorry you had to hide who you are. That is so unfair to you," she said.

"I know. I can't tell you how unhappy I was at times. But once I realized that it wasn't my fault and that God gave me many others things to be proud of, I was okay with it. I can't believe people actually think we choose to be this way." He flicked away a fallen tear. "I am sure there are some bisexuals that choose one way or another, but for the most part, most of us are born this way." He wiped at the sweat on his brow. "And I don't know of anything more scarier than the first time I realized I was different from others."

"Kade, you need to speak those exact words Wednesday night. You can still tell John's story, but I think if you add your own experience, it will make it even more personal and maybe people will be able to relate."

"Okay. I will do whatever you think that will help convince these people to vote for our proposal. We need to write down exactly what we are proposing." Kade grabbed a notebook and pen from the counter.

"I love you, son. I am so proud of you." She pulled up a chair and sat down. They spent the next few hours preparing for the upcoming meeting.

By the time they were ready to call it quits and go to bed, Monica was happy with all they had accomplished. She had a rush of self-confidence, something she hadn't felt until now. She knew she owed it all to Simon and Kade.

She was certain she wouldn't let her anger get the best of her at the meeting. She would fight this like a pro. She smiled as she cuddled up under the covers and said her prayers. She had to believe that this time they would listen.

Chapter Ten

Wednesday, July 9, 2008

Monica sat in the very same seat she sat last time. Only this time she had her son with her too. She felt good with Simon and Kade on each side of her. She knew they were the moral support that she needed.

Mr. Grisley started the meeting in the same manner he started the last meeting, going over all the old news first. As soon as he was done, he jumped straight to Monica's issue.

Monica could tell by the stern look in her eyes and his solemn face that he wasn't happy about her being there again.

"Monica Myers is joining us once again. Although her proposition was voted against, I have agreed to let her talk once last time because there were some issues that she didn't get to address last time." Stuart Grisley nodded toward Monica. "The floor is yours, Monica."

"Thank you, Mr. Grisley."

Mr. Grisley raised his hand, "We are on a first name basis here, remember? Please call me Stuart."

Monica had a strange sensation that Stuart wasn't going to be happy with anything she did. "Okay. Thanks.....*Stuart*." She proceeded to introduce Simon again and then Kade, explaining again all the accomplishments her son had achieved during high school. Then she added, "All the while, Kade knew he was gay and didn't have anyone to talk to about it. He hid it because he was scared people would be ashamed of him and think that he was a freak of some kind." She glanced toward Kade and then back at the audience. "If any of you are a mother or father, you can relate with how painful it is to see your child hurting for any reason." Her eyes watered. "It broke my heart, knowing my son had been struggling with his sexual identity and had to lie about who he was just so he wouldn't be taunted. No child should ever feel ashamed of who he or she it."

Monica, once again, went over statistics of gays but this time she added the suicide rate and told two horrid stories that had happened to two gay guys, e attempt. She ended her speech by saying, "I am aware that most of you are uncomfortable with homosexuality being taught in the schools during sex education. As a matter of fact, I can look across the room and tell most of you are uncomfortable just listening to me speak about it. And I guess if you aren't familiar with it and don't know anyone that is gay that may be why. But I guarantee there is someone that you know that is gay. A lot of homosexuals have not come forward to admit it, but there are a lot more of them than you think. If ten percent of human beings are gay that means there are at least fifty of them in your high school now."

Monica paused to sip her water. "It is time for us to step up and educate our children. I'm sure there is not one of you out there that wants your child to be taunted for any reason." She heard a few of them mumble no. "So how about we offer a different approach to help decrease the bullying of homosexuals in schools. First, we need to educate our students that it is natural for some to be attracted to the same sex and not to feel ashamed if they have those sorts of feelings. We need to emphasize to our children that they are not any less of a person if they find themselves attracted to the same sex. We need to teach the students that aren't gay how to respect the ones that are. The best way to do this is by educating the students about the homosexual community. Just as we educate the Africa Americans in February" She threw her hands in the air. "I know we can accomplish this if everyone would do their share and stick together as a team." She raised her voice, "We need to enforce even stricter policies in the schools. We need to let the students know that there will be zero tolerance against any type of discrimination."

"And what if we don't believe it *is* natural," A tall, heavy-set guy toward the back shouted out. Monica quickly realized it was the same guy that spoke out last time.

Monica bit her lip in anger and inhaled a deep breath before she spoke, "First off, this isn't matter of beliefs. There are innocent students killing themselves because adults would rather look the other way than to change the way they believe. And personally, I don't care about all the diversity beliefs in this world. The fact is that there are a large number of homosexuals in this world and still many that are afraid to come out and say it. And as long as people think the way that we do, there are many that will never feel safe to admit that they are gay."

She paused and took a few steps allowing time for the information to sink in. "And the one thing I *do* know is that no kid for any reason should be bullied! Every human life is valuable regardless if they are different." Monica glanced around the room to make sure she had everyone's attention. "My son has a powerful experience that he would like to share with you." She glanced back at Kade. "Would you please share John's story with us now?"

She didn't miss Stuart glancing at his watch.

Kade introduced himself once again and then told the most touching story of his friendship with John. He described everything that John had gone through with his father and how other boys had taunted him. He ended the story with John's suicide. Tears were streaming downs Kade's cheeks as he reached the end.

Monica glanced around the room and noticed a few tears from others too—especially Joan, the lovely lady that had lost her own sister to suicide due to bullying for being a lesbian. She was glad to see that John's story had touched many of them. Of course, Stuart's face remained somber and untouched by the story.

She thanked Kade and then addressed the room, "John was a very nice and likeable boy. And, I, too, will miss him dearly. This is why we have come up with a plan that we call 'John's Law' in honor of him. Basically, to start off with, we thought assemblies would be a great way to start getting the message across to students that the schools will not tolerate any bullying and to educate them more on the homosexual lifestyle."

Stuart quickly interrupted. "I don't know if you realize this, but unless you have volunteers, the school funding is low. More than likely, we wouldn't be able to add this into our budget."

Monica was quick to respond, although she wasn't quite sure of her own words. "I would be glad to do it. And I am sure I can get others to volunteer. You would be surprised to hear that there are many mothers and fathers out there that would be willing to step up to help if it could stop their children from being taunted for being gay."

Simon raised his hand. "I would help."

Joan also spoke up, "I would gladly volunteer. I agree with everything you have said today, Monica. And I hope everyone in this room realizes how important this is. We have to stop all this horrible taunting. You don't know how much I wish you would have been around, Monica, when my sister was alive. Thank you for what you are doing for our society."

Monica felt the applause around the room was more genuine this time around. "Thank you, Joan."

Stuart interrupted again. "Sorry, Monica, but we really need to wrap this up. We have other business to discuss. So if you don't have anything else to add."

"Just one more thing; I have sort of an outline of how the assembly could be run. Could I please leave this here for everyone to look at?" She glanced around the room. "Thank you all for allowing me to come back and talk again. I really hope you will think this through and vote yes for 'John's Law' so we can take a step toward ending bulling for once and for all. I am willing to do all the work and organization for it." She turned toward Stuart. "Thank you, Stuart."

"You're welcome. I will call you with the outcome."

"Okay, thanks." Monica gathered up her notes and handed Stuart the material for the group to look over.

She spun around and nodded to Kade and Simon. They followed her silently out the door.

As soon as she was outside she sighed heavily. "Wow, that was tough."

"I thought it went well," Simon commented.

"You did an amazing job," Kade said as he wrapped his arm around his mother's shoulder as they walked toward the car.

"Thanks. I couldn't have done it without you two." Monica crawled into the car. "I guess all we can do is wait and see." She glanced over her shoulder at Kade in the back seat. "I thought you did a remarkable job on John's story. It was very touching. And if they vote yes, I will have to give you the credit."

"Oh no, I can't take all the credit." He shrugged. "I just spoke from my heart which made it easier."

Simon agreed. "It was good, Kade. You both did an amazing job and should be proud. Even if it is voted against you can't hang your head. You did all you could do. If people want to be naïve and not see what is happening in our world, it is not our fault. We can try to change people, but sometimes they just won't budge."

"I know exactly what you are saying, Simon." Monica recalled Crystal's words about not being able to change society. It didn't seem fair that she could be fighting a losing battle, but she had to try. She just hoped she could handle the outcome if she failed to get her message across.

***

Monica immediately recognized the blue Impala parked directly behind her car in the driveway. A million thoughts raced through her head. "Great, what does he want?" She glanced toward Simon as he parked the car in front of the house. "It's Wayne."

"I figured, by the look on your face."

"Dad hasn't been around since he moved out." Kade glanced from his mom to Simon. "This can't be good. I am sure he hasn't changed his mind the way he feels about me."

Monica easily detected the hurt in Kade's voice. If only there was some way she could take away his pain.

She turned toward Simon. "Maybe, you shouldn't come in tonight." Her eyes met his. "I'm sorry. I just don't know what this is all about."

"It's okay. I understand. Call me later and let me know if everything is okay," Simon said.

Monica didn't wait for him to come around and open her door. She quickly climbed out of the car. "I will. Thanks, Simon. Talk to you later." She waited for Kade to climb out of the car and handed him the key to the house. "Maybe you ought to go on inside."

Kade glanced toward the rear of his dad's car and then back at his mom. "Okay, but I will be close to the door." He shrugged. "Just in case you need me or something."

"Thanks honey." She watched as Kade marched over to the house and unlocked the door. Not once did he glance his father's way.

As soon as the front door shut, Wayne leaped out of his car and started toward her. There was no need for her to approach him because he was already half way across the yard. She could tell by the look on his face that he wasn't happy either.

He immediately threw his hands up in the air. "What are you trying to prove, Monica?"

Monica's jaw dropped in surprise. "What are you talking about, Wayne?"

"I heard you have been going to the school board meetings, announcing to everyone that our son is gay."

She should have known it would eventually get back to him. "I am trying to help our son—unlike you!"

"Well, you sure know how to stir the pot. Do you know what this could do to my business?" He rested his hands on his hips. "I could lose hundreds of clients!"

Monica couldn't believe her ears. "And you think I care more about you losing clients than I do our son?" She shook her head. "Obviously, you don't know me very well!"

"Come on, Monica. You know I wouldn't do anything like this to ruin your reputation."

"My goal in life right now is not to ruin your reputation but to help others like Kade be accepted by their peers so they don't end up committing suicide like John did."

"John?" His forehead furrowed." Kade's faggot friend?"

"They are gay. Please don't call them that name or any others in front of me," she snapped. "Yes, his best friend, John.

"Well, I am sorry to hear that. But maybe it was for the best. I mean look at his life."

Monica's eyes narrowed. "Get out of my way. I have nothing more to say to you." She couldn't stand the sight of him anymore and the words that spurted out of his mouth made her want to puke.

Kade opened the door and stepped onto the porch. "Everything okay, Mom?" He shoved his hands into his jeans pockets.

"Yes, honey. Your dad was just leaving."

Wayne glared at Monica for a long moment. "This isn't the last you will hear from me." He spun away from her and marched back to his car. Never once did he look toward Kade who was still standing at the door. He jumped into his car and backed out of the driveway. He suddenly rolled down the window and yelled toward Monica, "I will mail you the divorce papers sometime this week." He rolled up the window and sped down the street.

Monica stared after him until he was out of sight. She turned toward Kade. "I am so sorry he is your father right now. I am so ashamed to have been married to a man that is so callous"

"Yeah, I'm pretty much a loser in his eyes. He will probably never want anything to do with me again."

"It is his loss, Kade." She hugged her son. "Please don't let him destroy the person you are. You are the best son a mother could have."

"Thanks, Mom." He pulled away from her. "I just wish he could accept me. It really hurts."

"I know it does, honey. It hurts me just as much. I know it has to bother you that he still wants to see Karmen." She opened the screen door. "I wish he was different too, sweetie." She nodded toward the kitchen. "Let's not let him ruin our day. I baked an apple pie earlier."

"Thanks Mom...for everything. I love you." Kade quickly pulled out a chair from the table. "Now let me sample that apple pie of yours and see if it is worth eating."

Monica laughed and before long they were enjoying the pie and discussing the events of the meeting.

Monica seemed to think Wayne was out of Kade's mind for the time, although the hurt would always be there.

She fought back the tears not wanting Kade to know how much the whole incident with his father had upset her. She wished there was a way she could take his pain away permanently.

Monica wished there was some way she could reassure all of the homosexuals that were struggling to be accepted in this hateful world! It just seemed so unfair!

Chapter Eleven

Thursday, July 10, 2008

Kade clocked out at work and hurriedly jerked his apron off as he made his way to his car. It seemed like the day had dragged on longer than usual. He couldn't seem to get his father and the recent incident of the night before out of his mind. He found himself holding back tears off and on all day long.

He wished there was some way he could make his father understand—but he knew it was useless. His father would never accept him. And it did bother him when his father would stop by the house to pick up Karmen for the weekend. Kade pretended it didn't hurt but there were many nights he'd cry himself to sleep.

He missed John and having a close friend to talk to. He felt like he could share anything with John.

He did meet a guy the night before from across town. They had planned to meet at Miss Gracie's Café for dinner and conversation. Miss Gracie's was a bar and grill downtown that was popular with the local gay community.

Kade had been there a couple of times with John and had met a few people but none that he had kept in contact with.

As he pulled up in front of the café, he made up his mind he wasn't going to try to have a good night and not think about John or the night before. He just needed to relax and meet some people that were more like him.

He entered through the door and was instantly greeted by a tall, feminine blond hair guy. "Welcome to Miss Gracie's. Would you like a table this evening?"

"Actually, I am meeting someone here." Kade glanced around the pink and lime green striped room and spotted Luke in a booth toward the back of the room. "There he is—over there." He pointed toward the booth.

The host led the way to the booth. "Your waiter is Jeremy and will be with you shortly."

"Thank you." Kade slid into the booth and offered his hand to Luke. "Your picture online doesn't do you justice." He shook his hand. "Nice to meet you, Luke."

"Thank you. Same here."

They placed their order and got acquainted as they waited for their food and drink to arrive.

Kade was quite impressed with Luke and his accomplishments so far. He was in his third year of college and was majoring in business. His goal was to have his own business within five years. He just wasn't certain what business he wanted to get involved in. He was leaning toward a having a restaurant only because it had been a longtime dream he had. He said his grandma had started teaching him to cook when he was just five years old, baking cookies and cakes. As the years went on, she taught him many of her secrets to baking all her delicious recipes.

"I don't know a thing about cooking. I guess my mom should have taught me some," Kade joked.

"My favorite thing to do is decorate wedding cakes. I have done a few for friends."

"How impressive," Kade added.

"I might consider a business in that line of work, also."

Kade was definitely glad the guy had ambition and was positive about his future. It was so different being around a gay guy that was content with his life than hanging around someone that was consistently depressed like John. Kade sort of felt guilty because he was having a good time. "Do you live with your grandma?"

"Yes, she raised me. And I couldn't have been more fortunate. I guess my mother ran off with her boyfriend a year after she had me, leaving me with Grams." Luke sipped his coke and continued. "She's never returned. Grams said she'd called a few times to check on me, but after a few years the calls got less and less frequent. Now, it has been seven years since she has called Grams. And Grams has no way of getting a hold of her. She would never leave a phone number."

"Wow, I am sorry." Kade was dumbfounded. He couldn't imagine a mother not wanting her son.

"Oh, it is no big deal. I never knew her so I never missed her. Grams was everything to me. Even when I told her I was gay a few years back; she just chuckled and said she had already assumed that many moons ago. She preached how that didn't make me any less of a person than a straight guy, and if I used that as a crutch for not succeeding in life, she would personally drag me through college and sit with me in every class." Luke laughed and rolled his eyes. "And if you knew Grams, you'd know she wasn't joking either."

"She sounds like an amazing lady." Luke waited while Jeremy refilled their sodas. "What about your father? Was he the man your mother ran off with?"

Luke laughed. "Are you kidding? Grams said she'd gone through four different boyfriends in the year that she did live at home. She never would tell Grams who my father was. Grams doesn't even she really knew herself."

"I bet she was young when she had you," Kade guessed.

"Bingo! Yeah, she was sixteen and not at all ready to raise a child."

"I bet she has regrets now."

Luke stuffed the rest of his hamburger in his mouth and finished chewing. "Yeah, maybe. It really doesn't bother me. I am thrilled that Grams was the one to raise me. She's the best. You will have to meet her."

"I would like that."

"Enough about me—tell me more about your family." Luke wiped his mouth with a napkin and tossed it in his plate.

Kade spent the next twenty minutes telling Luke everything he could think of that might seem interesting. He spoke highly of his mother and not so highly of his father. He told Luke about John and how devastated he was to learn he'd taken his own life. He told Luke all about the board meeting him and his mom had attended and what they hoped to achieve by doing so.

"I think that is so awesome," Luke said.

"Yeah, I'm pretty stoked about it myself. I feel like I am doing something for John." His eyes clouded. "Just wish I could have done something for him earlier."

"Hey, you can't blame yourself for his suicide. It sounds like he was terribly depressed. Sooner or later he would have ended his life regardless of what you should've or even could've done to help."

Luke's words meant a lot to Kade for some odd reason. Maybe it was because he was gay himself and he was telling him there wasn't a thing he could have done to have prevented it. "Thanks, that means a lot." Kade had just assumed since he was gay that there could have been something that he could have said or done to persuade John not to do it.

It seemed like one conversation led to another and Kade was glad that Luke was so easy to talk to. And the good looks just seemed to be a bonus.

He glanced at the floral clock across the room as he laughed at a remark Luke had made. "Wow, I can't believe we have been here two hours."

"Holy crap! Sorry—Grams would scold me for using those two words together." He laughed. "I need to scoot. I have so much homework to do."

"Yeah, my mother is probably freaking out herself." He paid Jeremy after arguing with Luke who was going to pay.

"Okay, I can tell you're pretty stubborn." Luke laughed. "I got it next time." He paused. "Um…that is if you want to get together again."

"Yeah, I would like that. I had a great time tonight," Kade walked with Luke toward his car. "Maybe we can do something this weekend?"

"Sounds great to me!" Luke said. "Oh wait—I can't this weekend, I have my niece's birthday party Saturday night. But maybe during the week we can go out to eat or something."

They quickly exchanged phone numbers and Kade told Luke he'd give him a call in a couple days.

Kade climbed in his Cougar excited about the positive connection he'd made with Luke. Finally he'd met someone that he might potentially be interested in something more than friendship. He'd been waiting a long time to feel sparks for someone, and he was certain this was the beginning of a good thing.

He pressed on the gas pedal and spun out of the parking lot. He couldn't wait to get home and share his evening events with his new best friend—his mom.

***

Sunday, July 13, 2008

Monica couldn't believe it. She slammed the phone down. Stuart just called and said that their proposal had passed. "We did it!" She yelled.

She glanced down at her trembling hands—she'd been so nervous when she realized it was him. She hadn't been expecting Stuart since it was Sunday morning. She'd just assumed it was someone trying to sell something because that was usually the only calls she got on her landline phone. She shrugged her shoulders. *Who cares*, she thought, *as long as he called*. "And it passed!" she shouted into the silent, empty house. Kade had already left for work, and Karmen had spent the night with Mindy.

"I can't believe it!" She wished one of the kids were home so she could share the good news with them. She grabbed her cell phone and called Simon.

After a couple rings, he answered. "Good morning, beautiful."

"Why thank you, Simon. It is definitely going to be a beautiful day," Monica announced.

"Any other reason besides the glorious sun shining?"

"We did it! Mr. Grisley called and they voted for our proposal."

"You're kidding? Monica, that is awesome news!"

"I know. I know. I'm so excited right now. I wish Kade was here for me to tell."

"I'm so proud of you." Simon paused. "You really have your work cut out for you now. I hope you will still have time for me?"

"Of course I will, silly." She plopped down in the chair. Her adrenaline suddenly increased. "Wow, I have a lot to do before school starts. And I have to find some help." She sighed. "I guess I should have asked about getting off work first. I guess I just assumed it wouldn't pass."

"Calm down. You're getting rattled. It will all fall together. If you want, I can come over this afternoon and help you put a plan together. "

"Simon, that would be a big help."

"I even know a few people I could call that I'm pretty sure would help us."

"I really appreciate it. I was so excited, I didn't even think about all the work I had to do," she said.

"Don't worry about it. Sit down and drink a cup of coffee and gather your thoughts. I'll be over in a couple of hours and we'll get started on it. You will do fine, Monica."

"Thanks. You're the best. See you shortly." She hung up the phone as a thousand thoughts raced through her head. She was thankful that she had Simon to help her sort through all of the chaos. She wasn't quite sure were to start.

But first, she was going to take Simon's advice and drink another cup of coffee while enjoying a few minutes of her victory. She couldn't wait to tell Kade. She quickly texted him and told him to call her on his break. She didn't want to send the news through a text—she wanted to hear his voice when she told him the news. She knew he would be thrilled and proud—and he deserved to be both.

She suddenly squeezed her eyes shut and prayed out loud. "Thank you, Lord. I know one day things will be different for homosexuals all around the world—I'm aware, though, that it is just a slow process. Please give me the patience I need to carry this forward and please keep leading me in the right direction. Amen."

***

Later:

Kade couldn't believe it when his mother told him 'John's Law' had passed. He was so glad that he was a part of the process and had the opportunity to share John's story. He was sure that had helped convince some of the members.

He briefly thought of John and the last time they had hung out. He remembered the first time he took John to ride horses and how excited he'd been. Kade recalled him saying that he wished he had somewhere like that to go to every time he got upset.

Kade remembered the pain he felt when he found out that John had died and there was nothing more that he could do. It still saddened him that he hadn't been able to convince his friend differently. He hadn't even had a chance to talk to him.

He wasn't quite sure why he was so adamant about helping 'John's Law' go into effect, but in the back of his mind, he realized it was important. Not only important to him and the fact that he felt a little guilty for what happened to John, but for all the people struggling with the same issue. He was sure that if John wasn't bullied so much at school and treated so badly at home that he would be alive and with him today. At this point, there was nothing he could do to save John—but he felt it was his obligation to spread John's story to prevent it from happening again.

Kade glanced at his watch—6:00 p.m. He told the checker goodbye and headed to the back of the store.

He thought of his mom and all the hard work she'd been doing lately on this project. She meant the world to him and he knew that she loved him more that anyone ever could. He was so fortunate to have her as a mother. He was so proud of her and all that she was doing to help the gay community.

He sort of wished he'd chosen a nearby college to go to this fall so he could help his mom out. He immediately thought of Luke. He realized if something did become of them, a long distant relationship would be tough. But he'd come back for all the holidays, so maybe it wouldn't be too difficult. He hadn't been expecting to meet someone right before he went off to college. He shook his head as he clocked out and slid the time card into the slot. He was always trying to see into the future instead of just letting each day just happen. He'd only met the guy one time and he was already dreaming up a future with him. He chuckled silently. That was the Sagittarius in him. *We are such dreamers,* he thought.

He pulled off his apron, draped it over his arm, and hurried out of the store.

Dale was climbing out of his car and called out. "Hey, I work with you tomorrow."

"Awesome. Don't work too hard tonight." Kade marched toward his own car, which was parked at the very back of the parking lot.

He glanced around the parking lot—it was nearly vacant. Most of the weekend shoppers had already gotten their groceries.

He glanced toward his car. There was a guy leaning against it. He was still too far away to make out who it was. He assumed it was one of the workers wanting to gossip about work or something.

His eyes widened and his pace slowed as he drew closer to the figure. He stared ahead in shock. His heart felt like it was stuck in his throat and just breathing seemed difficult. Kade sensed something was very wrong and suddenly he was nervous. The hairs on his arms stiffened as bad vibes ran through his veins. He had a crushing feeling that it was going to be a very bad evening.

Chapter Twelve

Later: 11:00 P.M.

Monica walked to the living room window and peered out into the empty streets. She had repeated the same steps over and over for the last four hours. She'd walk to the table, take a drink of soda, and then back to the window to look up and down the streets to see if Kade's car was anywhere in view.

The uneaten hamburgers and baked potatoes were still sitting on the table. Karmen had come and gone to go eat pizza with her friends earlier in the evening. Not long after, she had called and asked to stay all night at Mindy's again. Any other time, Monica would have said no since she'd already stayed the night before. But this time she didn't want Karmen to see how worried she was about Kade, so she'd agreed to it.

Monica paced nervously in front of the big bay window. She'd already drawn the drapes back to make the street more visible. She sighed impatiently and whirled around to snatch her cell phone off the end table. She tried calling Kade's phone again, although she was certain she would get his voice mail just like she had numerous times before. And she was right—straight to his voice mail which either meant his phone was turned off or dead. "Damn it, Kade. Where the hell are you?" She yelled into the silent phone.

She tossed the cell phone on the chair, frustrated. She knew this wasn't like Kade at all. He always called if he wasn't coming home for dinner. She'd already called his job and they confirmed that he had clocked out at six.

Monica's cell phone rang and she jumped. "Thank God!" She was certain it had to be Kade. She glanced down at the phone number and her heart sunk. It was just Karmen. "Hello, honey," she said, disappointed.

"Mom, you told me to call when we got to Mindy's and I forgot earlier. But I promised we have been home for awhile."

"Oh, that's fine, honey. Thanks for letting me know."

"Why's Kade working so late? Is he pulling a double for someone?"

Monica's heart skipped a beat. "What are you talking about?"

"We drove by Price Chopper on our way home and his car was still there."

"It is?" Monica asked. "That's odd," she muttered to herself.

"He didn't call you?"

Monica knew she couldn't hide the truth from Karmen. "No, and I have been worried sick about him." Her voice cracked. She was trying to hold it together. "I called his work and they said he clocked out at six."

"Well, maybe, whoever you talked to didn't know he was filling in for someone. And his phone could be dead again. You know how he's always forgetting to charge it at night."

121

"Yeah, maybe." *It did make sense*, Monica thought. "You'd think he would have borrowed someone's phone and called me to let me know."

"He's just not as dependable as I am," she teased. "I think you should ground him."

"Oh Karm, I'm being serious. I am worried."

"I'm sorry, Mom. I'm sure he'll be home soon."

"I don't know," Monica wandered to the window again and stared out at the deserted street. "I'm going to drive down to the store myself."

"If you are really that concerned, I'll come home. Stay put and I'll go with you."

"You don't have to do that," Monica said, although she was secretly hoping Karm would go with her.

"I want to. You sound too upset to drive anyway. I can drive you down there."

"Okay, honey, thanks. See you in a bit."

Monica crossed the room and grabbed her purse. She stuffed her phone inside and set it on the coffee table. She glanced down at what she was wearing—a faded t-shirt and a pair of old cut-off shorts that she'd had for several years.

She planned on going to the police if she couldn't find Kade at the store. Her eyes filled with tears. "Dear God, please let him be at work," she prayed as she dashed into the bedroom to change.

She quickly threw on some jeans and a nicer shirt and hurried back into the living room to wait for Karmen. She couldn't help but notice her hands were trembling as she picked up her purse. She'd worried plenty of times about the children in the past but she didn't remember ever being *this* nervous about either of them. She knew Kade would have called her regardless of where he was or what he was doing. Something just wasn't adding up. He'd been so excited when he'd called on his break and she had told him about the news from Mr. Grisley.

She suddenly recalled him saying he'd help her when he got off. She was certain if he had to work later that he would have known by then. "Oh God," she moaned. *But maybe someone got sick at the last minute and he didn't know he had to work.*

She took a deep breath. She needed to calm down before Karmen got there. She bowed her head and prayed like she had never prayed before.

***

Later: 1:10 A.M.

Monica walked around Kade's car again for the fifth time, looking for any kind of clues that might give her a lead tell her where her son had gone.

She'd already walked the aisles of Price Chopper and talked to all of the employees that were working. They assured her that Kade had clocked out at six. One of the carry-outs named Dale told her that Kade was just leaving as he was coming to work. He'd assured her that he had last seen him walking toward his car that was parked in the back of the parking lot.

None of it made sense to Monica. She squatted on her knees and looked underneath his car. She wasn't sure what she was looking for but didn't know what else to do.

She poked her head in the car at Karmen who was busy sorting through Kade's glove compartment. "Find anything?" Monica was glad she had always insisted on keeping a spare key for Kade's car in her purse.

"No, nothing," Karmen replied.

"I can't believe the police won't take a report for 24 hours." Monica had phoned the police earlier and a policeman named Bob told her that Kade was probably with a bunch of friends and lost track of the time. He told her that Kade would probably show up after a while. He preached about the numerous calls they receive nightly from parents looking for their teenagers. And nine out of ten times they always show up with a lame excuse. Bob told her to give it until at least tomorrow and then, if Kade still hadn't showed up, she could come down and file a missing report. He continued to reassure her that he would probably be home before morning. He had chuckled and asked whether she'd contacted his girlfriend. Monica replied that Kade was gay and didn't have a boyfriend at the time. It didn't take but a second for the chuckling to cease and he, once again, told her not to worry so much.

"Luke," she suddenly said out loud as she thumped the side of her head.

"What?" Karmen asked.

"The guy Kade met on the Internet and went to dinner with the other night. His name was Luke—but I can't remember what he said his last name was."

"Oh yeah, he was talking to him on the phone last night," Karmen added. "Maybe he is with him."

"Why wouldn't he call me, though?" Monica pulled her cell phone out of her jean's pocket and tried Kade's cell again. Again it went to his voicemail. This time she left a message telling him to call her as soon as possible. "It's just not like him." She shook her head as she climbed in behind Kade's steering wheel.

"Maybe we can find Luke's last name in Kade's room somewhere." Karmen pushed the glove compartment closed. "Nothing there!" She glanced around the car. "He's such a clean freak. There isn't even an empty water bottle in this car."

Monica smiled as she glanced around the car. She could faintly smell his favorite cologne—Obsession. "He's always been a perfectionist—unlike you." She grinned. She always teased Karmen about her messy room.

"Well, at least I call and tell you where I am," Karmen mocked back. "Mom, let's go home. I'm sure he's okay. I'll bet he is with that Luke guy. They talked forever last night."

"Yeah, maybe you are right. He has been out this late before. He just usually lets me know. Maybe he was just rushed and it slipped his mind. Or maybe he didn't want Luke to know he had to call his mommy." Monica tried to believe her own words but was still unconvinced.

Karmen added, "Or maybe his phone did die and he was embarrassed to ask Luke to use his phone to call you." She smiled and rubbed her mom's hand. "He'll show up, Mom."

Monica nodded. "You're right. I am just being paranoid." She climbed out of the car. "Let's go home," She stated as she locked Kade's car. "But I'm not sleeping until I hear from him."

"Sure, Mom." Karmen climbed back in her own car and fired up the engine.

Monica rode in silence all the way home. *Who was this Luke guy,* she wondered. She was always reading horror stories of girls that meet men on the Internet. *Was it possible that men could be in just as much danger as girls?*

Earlier she'd imagine Kade possibly getting in a car wreck but now her mind was wandering to even more bizarre situations. Goosebumps surfaced across her arms. She didn't like where her thoughts were heading.

She had to think positive or she would drive herself insane. She leaned her head back against the headrest and squeezed her eyes shut. *He'll be home soon,* she told herself. She had to believe that—she had to.

***

Monday, July 14, 2008, 3:00 a.m.

Kade rubbed his eyes as he tried to clear his head. He felt disorientated. It was so dark. He knew he was lying on a bed; he just didn't know where. He lifted his head but was too dizzy to make out anything. "Anybody here?" he whispered, weakly. "Help me, please." Just speaking drained him. He quickly dropped his head back down and closed his eyes. He didn't think anyone could hear him anyway, which frightened him even more.

He had no clue where he was or how he had gotten there. His memory was so blurred and his head was pounding with pain. He couldn't even think which day of the week it was. *What has happened to me,* he wondered. "Where the hell am I?" he muttered softly. He forced his eyes opened and rolled his head to the side. He stared into the darkness—he thought he could vaguely make out a brick wall. He rolled his head to the other side, but his vision blurred again. He blinked and opened his eyes. His eyes slowly focused. It looked to be an outline of a dresser of some sort pushed up against the wall.

Again, he struggled with trying to remember how he had gotten there. He recalled drinking something. It was a fountain drink of some sort. Someone had given him something to drink. He couldn't recall who gave it to him though—but it was the last thing he could remember.

"Please help me," he called out again with a stronger voice.

Kade listened but couldn't even hear a clock ticking or an air condition humming. It was way too quiet.

Suddenly he remembered being at work and clocking out. It was slowly coming back to him. It was Sunday and he'd worked all day. He had called his mom on his break and she had told him that 'John's Law' had passed. He'd been anxious to get off work and get home to start the research.

His eyes closed—he was so tired. Just trying to remember was so exhausting. He started to doze off. He remembered the drink again. It tasted like Dr. Pepper but different for some reason. It had made him so sleepy. He could see the hands of the guy. They looked so familiar but the face was blurred. *Who was it?* He struggled to see an image. He sensed something was peculiar about the whole incident. He was certain whoever gave him the drink had bad intentions.

His eyes suddenly flew open. He remembered. "Oh my God," he said out loud. He knew who gave him the drink. He could now see the hands handing him the drink and the smile across his face. He remembered seeing him leaning against his car as he walked from the store. He recalled the kindness in his eyes—but mostly he remembered the sincerity in his voice.

Kade's eyes watered as the image in his head grew stronger. "Oh, God," he cried softly. "Why?"

Chapter Thirteen

Monday, July 14, 8:10 a.m.

Monica poured the last of the coffee into her mug. It was the second pot she'd made since she arrived home. Karmen had gone to bed hours ago, insisting that Monica wake her if she heard anything from Kade.

Monica glanced down at her cell phone, hoping somehow she'd missed a phone call from him; she hadn't. It had been hours since Kade had gotten off work and still there had been no word from him. She even called the police again to make sure there hadn't been any reports anywhere that might have involved Kade. The police had informed her that it had been a quiet night, and if she wanted, she could come down in the morning and file a report if he hadn't showed up through the night.

Frantically, she called Simon and explained the situation. He scolded her for not contacting him sooner. He insisted on taking off early and going with her to the police station. He said he would be there as soon as he could.

She thought she should call Wayne and let him know the circumstances, but she just couldn't bring herself to do it—

at least not yet. After the way he had treated Kade these last few weeks, she really didn't think he would be too concerned about his son missing. But maybe he would have a change of heart, but she doubted it.

She took a sip of the coffee, set the mug on the table, and hurried down the hallway toward Kade's room. She'd searched earlier trying to find Luke's last name or a phone number but hadn't come up with anything. She hadn't thought to look on Kade's computer. The fatigue had started settling in earlier, and she was sure that was why she wasn't able to think clearly.

She quickly booted up the computer and entered Facebook's web address. She had an account with Facebook but rarely logged into it. She quickly logged in and went to her home page. She found Kade's profile from her friends list and clicked on it. *Bingo!* Sure enough Luke had left him a couple of comments. She quickly clicked on Luke's profile and was able to get the information she needed—Luke Goodloe. He even had his phone number listed.

She jumped up and ran to retrieve her cell phone. She rushed back and quickly dialed the number. The phone rang several times before going to his voice mail. She left a quick message, explaining who she was and why she was calling. She asked him if he would please return her call as soon as possible.

"Damn," she mumbled as she hung up. She was disappointed that he hadn't answer. She was certain that Luke could help her locate Kade.

She spent the next two hours going over Luke's profile and other friends of Kade's, trying to find anything unusual that could lead her to her son.

Her cell phone rang, startling her. She snatched it up and immediately recognized Luke's phone number. "Hello."

"Hi. Mrs. Myers?"

"Yes, it is. Is this Luke Goodloe?"

"Yes, ma'am."

"I am so sorry I called you so early. But I have looked everywhere for Kade and was hoping that maybe you had seen him." Monica twisted her hair around her index finger as she waited nervously for Luke's respond.

"Oh, wow! That explains why he hasn't called me. I haven't talked to him since Saturday night. He was supposed to call me last night when he got off work, but I never heard from him."

"Oh!" Monica couldn't tell if the kid was telling the truth or not. If only she could see his face, she was certain she would be able to tell if he was lying. Suddenly she had an idea, she'd try bluffing him. "Well, I have to make a police report shortly. The police will probably be contacting you to ask questions. Is this a good number for them to reach you?"

"Yes, of course. I can meet you down at the station if you want. I am concerned myself. I really like your son, Mrs. Myers."

"Please, call me Monica. That would be great. I will give you a call as soon as I leave here."

"I really hope everything is okay. Would you please call me if you hear from him?"

"I will. Thanks Luke." She hung up the phone, convinced the kid was being sincere. But she wouldn't know for certain until she met him face to face. She could pinpoint a liar in a room full of people any day. She'd always been gifted in that way.

She instantly thought of Kade and quickly made an exception. She hadn't been able to tell with him. She recalled all of the years he'd pretended to be straight, and she never had a clue. She imagined that when someone has such a huge secret to cover up, as Kade did, it was easier to pull off. And the fact that he'd been doing it for years probably made it easier. It still saddened Monica when she thought of his early years and what he must have went through; taking such a heavy burden on all alone at such a young age must have been devastating.

Monica spent the next hour going through Kade's files on his computer to see if there was anything that could link him to his whereabouts.

She glanced at her watch and realized it was after eleven and Simon would be showing up shortly to take her to the police station. She quickly showered and changed her clothes.

Monica debated whether to wake Karmen or not. The doorbell rang and she was certain in was Simon. She decided to leave Karmen a note that she'd gone to the police station with Simon. She knew there wasn't much Karmen could do if she woke her up.

She quickly scribbled a note and left it on the table. She snatched up her purse and hurried toward the door.

Monica yanked the door open. Just seeing Simon standing there overwhelmed her. She rushed into his arms and sobbed. "Oh, God, he still has never shown up. I am so scared that he is hurt somewhere."

Simon patted her head gently. "Hey. Calm down, sweetie. We will find him. I promise you." He pulled her away from him and stared into her swollen eyes, "You should have called me last night. I care about you tremendously. I want to help. I promise I will be right by

your side until he shows up. I am here for you to lean on."
He lifted her chin. "Do you understand?"

"Yes, Simon. Thank you so much." He bent down and
brushed her lips with his own. Even though it was a sincere
kiss rather than a passionate kiss, Monica couldn't control
the tingling feeling it had created. At that second she knew
she was falling in love with him.

Simon grabbed her hand. "Come on; let's go find your
son."

Monica knew that no more words were necessary. She
knew how he felt about her and she was sure he knew how
she felt. "Simon, I am really scared. I have never been this
scared in my life." The tears rowed down her cheeks.

Simon pulled away from the curb as he rubbed her hand.
"I know you are. I am praying like crazy for Kade's safe
return home. We have to keep the faith that he is okay."

"I am trying so hard." She squeezed her eyes shut tightly
to block all the horrible images floating through her head.
Please, God, let him be okay, she prayed silently.

***

Monica had called Luke on the way to the station. He
had shown up just like he'd promised. He sat through the
whole interrogation with her and Simon while they filed a
report. He had politely answered all the questions the police
had asked. And Monica didn't think he acted the least bit
suspicious. She was certain he was being sincere on all
levels.

As they walked toward their vehicles, Monica studied
Luke. He was tall and average built. His hair was the color
of milk chocolate and cut short in a fashionable manner—

parted toward the side. She was extremely impressed with his manners—such a well-mannered kid.

She suddenly recalled some of the detective shows she watched on TV, and how the best-behaved men would end up being the worst criminals. She quickly wondered if Luke could fall into this category.

Monica quickly discarded the idea. She knew she was being paranoid. She just couldn't see Luke being mean to anyone. She could easily understand why Kade was attracted to him. He was a kind, nice looking young man.

They stopped at Luke's car, and Monica extended her hand toward him. "It was very nice to meet you, Luke. Thank you so much for meeting us down here."

"Why of course, Monica. I, too, am very concerned about Kade. And it was my pleasure meeting you." Luke shook Monica's hand and then Simon's. "And you too, Simon."

"I don't know what to do next," Monica glanced awkwardly around the parking lot.

"I know what you mean. I don't think I will accomplish much today until Kade is found." Luke opened his car door. "Would you please call me as soon as you hear anything?"

"I sure will," Monica said.

Simon interrupted. "Or I will call you. I'm going to try to get Monica to sleep for a while." He glanced at Monica as if to finalize that *no* would not be an option.

"You do look tired, Monica," Luke added.

"Oh I am. I am drained. But I know there is no way I can sleep until I know Kade is safe."

Simon winked at Luke. "Oh, I can find her a way to sleep." He smiled warmly at Monica. "Seriously, you need rest so you'll have your strength when Kade does return home."

Monica needed to hear those words *'when Kade does return home'*. It was almost an assurance that he'd be home soon. "I know that you're right, and I will try."

Monica waved to Luke as he climbed into his own car. She prayed the kid was being genuine. She grabbed Simon's hand as she walked to the car. "I couldn't do this alone. Thank you so much for staying with me."

"I am not leaving your side until Kade is found. I told you that. My job is flexible enough—they don't need me there."

"That means everything to me, Simon." She waited for Simon to unlock the door. "You know I am going to have to call Wayne and let him know about this." She knew that Simon was well aware of the situation with Wayne and how he had treated Kade.

"I know you don't want to, Monica. But that is something you will have to do sooner or later."

She sighed heavily and glanced out the window. "I know. I will call him as soon as I get home." She was certain he would try to turn the situation around and try to make it appear to be all her fault. He was good at that.

They rode the rest of the way home in silence as Monica's mind wandered about Kade's whereabouts.

***

Kade stirred awake as the voices grew closer. He'd been hoping that he'd been dreaming and the dark room would actually be his bedroom when he woke. He glanced around the gloomy room, confirming that he wasn't delusional.

The dizziness had subsided and his memory became clearer. He could hear the voices now outside his door but couldn't make out what they were saying.

The memory of the night before was not a dream. It was real and the man that had brought him to this horrific place was none other than his own father. He recalled how his dad had been leaning against his car after he'd got off work. He'd told Kade that he wanted to make peace and they needed to talk.

Kade had been hesitant at first, but his dad had seemed so sincere that he agreed to talk with him. Deep inside, Kade had been ecstatic that his dad was trying to make amends with him.

As soon as he crawled into his father's car, his dad had offered him a Dr. Pepper and said, "It's your favorite."

Kade had been touched by his father's gesture and had eagerly started drinking the soda, savoring the presence of his father and not realizing how much he'd missed him.

Kade remembered how his vision blurred as his father rattled on and on, about how all he wanted was what was best for him, and how one day he would thank him for doing what he had to do. Kade recalled the more his dad talked the less sense he was making and the more tired he grew. The last thing he remembered was his father driving away from the city.

He didn't remember a thing after that or how long he'd been in this dreary room. He was certain, however, that it *was* his father who had brought him here.

Suddenly, the door flew open and a trio of two elderly men and a middle-age woman gathered around his bed. They immediately clasped hands and started chanting in a language Kade couldn't recognize.

He tried to sit up but the fiery red-haired lady motioned him to lie back down. Once again, they continued their chanting. Finally, after several minutes, they grew quiet.

They bowed their heads, closed their eyes, and seemed to be praying.

Kade was shocked by the chaos circling him and was clueless as to what in the heck was going on. He was almost too scared to speak. Finally he mustered up the courage, "Who are you guys? And why am I here?" He glanced toward the elderly guy with glasses and long dark beard, "Where is my dad?"

The guy squinted briefly as he studied Kade, and then his beady eyes widened. "We are going to save you from Satan before it is too late. Your father believes you can be cured and so do we. Through your prayers and your faith, you can turn your life around and lead a normal life as one of Jesus' children."

Kade was speechless. How could he have had trusted his father to love him for who he was? He was devastated—it felt like his heart had been shattered. He let the tears stream down his face—he was certain life would never be the same again.

Suddenly, all he could think about was his mom and how he wished he was young again and snuggled up in her arms. He didn't even realize he was crying out loud, "I want my mom," he begged. "I want my mom!"

Chapter Fourteen

Later: 4:30 p.m.

Monica knew she couldn't put off calling Wayne any longer. It was *his* son after all.

"Okay, here it goes," she told Simon as she picked up her cell phone.

Wayne answered after one ring, "Hello."

Monica took a deep breath. "Wayne, its Monica," *Duh,* she thought, she'd called his cell phone after all. He'd have to know who it was. "Ummm, I am afraid I have some bad news?"

"Oh?"

"It's about Kade. He never made it home from work yesterday. His car was found still in the parking lot at Price Chopper." Monica listened to Wayne's shallow breathing while wondering what was taking him so long to comment.

Finally, Wayne spoke, "Well, maybe he is with friends?" He sighed. "You know you were always such a worry wart, Monica. I am sure he is fine."

Bastard, she wanted to scream. "Seriously, Wayne! I am not exaggerating. He is not with any friends. I have called everyone I could possibly think of."

"I think there is a lot your son has been hiding from you, Monica. I think you are blind to what is going on in his life."

"He is *your* son too, you know," she spat out. "How can you be so callous?" She was getting angrier by the second. She glanced toward Simon and rolled her eyes.

Simon shook his head as if he completely understood why she was upset.

"Calm down, Monica. All I am saying is that he is probably fine. He probably went out, stayed up late, and crashed at someone's house."

"I don't think so, Wayne. But of course that is what you would think."

"If he is not home by this evening, why don't you call the police station?" Wayne asked.

"I've already done that."

"We'll see. You have nothing to worry about then. If something was wrong, the police would have contacted you. Not to change the subject, but did Karm tell you I was picking her up later to go out for dinner."

What an ass, Monica thought. "Yeah, she mentioned it. But with Kade missing and all, I'm not sure what her plans are now."

"Well, there's not much she can do, anyway," Wayne added.

"She's upset, Wayne. Did you ever consider that?"

"Okay, okay. I don't feel like arguing with you. I will just give her call and see what her plans are."

Monica, annoyed, asked, "Would you like me to call and let you know if Kade shows up?" She had to bite her lower lip to keep from giving him a real piece of her mind.

"Sure, I'd appreciate it. But don't beat yourself up over this. I am sure he is fine. Talk to you later, Monica."

"Bye!" She was scared to say much else—in fear that she would say more than she should. She didn't know why she really cared except she had to keep in mind that Karmen still had a good relationship with her father.

"I'm sorry, Monica," Simon said as soon as she got off the phone.

Monica heard Karmen's cell phone ringing in her bedroom and was certain it was Wayne. He didn't waste any time calling Karm but could care less if Kade was dead or alive.

"What a jerk," Monica whispered so Karmen couldn't hear.

"I am so sorry that Kade has a father like that," Simon whispered back.

"Yeah, me too!" She dropped down in the kitchen chair.

"Wait a minute. You promised me you'd lie down as soon as you called Wayne. Do you have any sleeping medicine to help you fall asleep?"

She jumped to her feet and threw her arms around Simon's neck. "You're too good to be true. Thank you for everything." She squeezed him tight. "Yes, I will lie down but I don't want to take anything. And you have to promise me you will wake me if anyone calls about anything."

"Okay, I will."

"Promise?" Monica kissed him lightly on the lips. "I am so tired."

"I promise—and I'll be right here when you get up."

"Thanks, Simon. Help yourself to anything. See you shortly. Don't let me sleep too long."

Monica stopped at Karmen's room before going to her own. She was glad that Karmen had agreed to go eat dinner with her father. Maybe it would take her mind off things for awhile.

"Call me, Mom, if Kade calls."

"I will, sweetie. Have a good dinner." Monica kissed her daughter on the cheek. "And be careful," she quickly added. She knew if anything else happened to her family, she'd lose it.

All she could think about was collapsing in her bed and letting some of the emotions out that had been building up. She'd been fighting back the tears for the last few hours. She needed some alone time now and a little shut eye might do her some good.

***

Kade kneeled at the pew like he was instructed to do. Although he didn't think he was in an actual church, the room was set up like a sanctuary.

He did as he was told—too afraid of the consequences if he didn't.

The short, chubby guy had smacked him across the face when he'd cried for his mother earlier. The guy had screamed, "You will not cause trouble while you are here. Do you understand?" The shock and the sting from the slap made him realize just how serious these people were.

Kade glanced toward the red- haired lady as she moved toward the podium. He guessed the woman to be in her mid-forties. She was a big-boned woman; not heavy, but built stocky. Her hands were big and looked powerful like hands of a man. Her hair was chopped short and slicked back.

Kade found it ironic that she fit so many stereotypes of a lesbian as this was the lady who was trying to convince him that Jesus could change him. At this point, thinking of silly things was all that Kade could do to try and stay sane.

The lady took a position behind the podium. The men had called her Cindy. She pulled a cross on a chain from a drawer and slid it around her neck.

The other two men knelt on each side of Kade and bowed their heads.

Kade had heard the chubby one call the guy with the glasses, Marion. He wasn't sure, yet, what the plump fellow was called. Although Marion had called him Buddy once, Kade wasn't sure if that was his name or just a figure of speech.

Suddenly, Cindy started chanting in a different language again and the men repeated a few of the words in the chant.

Kade kept his head bowed, untouched and confused by the whole scenario. He wasn't sure what they were trying to prove but to him they just looked crazy.

Cindy glanced toward the ceiling and then toward Kade. She suddenly changed her language to English. "Dear Father, please hear our prayers. We need your help. We have a young man with us today that Satan is trying to take over. He has turned against you, Lord, and is doing acts of the devil."

Kade tried to swallow the lump in his throat. He couldn't believe the words he was hearing. He was having a hard time keeping quiet. He wanted to tell this foolish woman how nuts she sounded.

Cindy's eyes met Kade's. "I know you are confused, son. I was once in your same shoes but, through prayer, I have been saved and you can be too."

"I am a Christian," Kade said bluntly. "I am a gay Christian," he added.

"God doesn't like gays," Cindy said. "That is the devil talking through you."

"If God doesn't like us, how come he has made so many of us?" Kade knew he could easily debate this dim-witted woman if given the chance. She hadn't a clue what she was talking about.

Marion quickly nudged Kade hard in the ribs. "Just be quiet and listen to her. You are not to speak."

Although the jab hurt, Kade spoke out anyway, "You believe this nonsense?" Kade glanced from Marion to Buddy. He immediately could tell by the reactions on their faces that they believed her nonsense. Within just a few seconds, they all three looked crazy as hell. And Kade couldn't help but wonder just how irrational these people could be.

Buddy spoke up, "One more word from you and you will go without dinner."

The furthest thing from Kade's mind was dinner. All he cared about was getting the hell out of this nutty place. He couldn't believe his father brought him here. Surely he had no idea what these people were like.

How could anyone really believe that prayer could make you straight? Cindy probably thought prayer made her straight because she was in denial about her sexuality. But her attractions toward women would never diminish entirely. She would just go through life covering up her desires and live a very unhappy life, thinking that is what God wanted her to do.

Kade didn't believe, for one moment, that God would make him gay and then tell him not to act upon it or he would be a sinner. After all, God is not evil.

Kade wasn't going to change his beliefs for some wacky lady that tells him he is going to Hell if he doesn't. He didn't care what these idiots tried to do to him. He was going to stay true to who he was if it was the last thing he did.

Marion and Buddy both went back to mumbling in their foreign language. Kade wasn't even sure it was a language. He'd never heard anything like it before.

Cindy's overpowering voice boomed across the room. "Pray with us, son, if you want to be forgiven of your sins."

Kade was furious. "I'm leaving. You can't keep me here against my will." He stood—but Marion and Buddy immediately grabbed his arms.

Buddy frowned. "We warned you, boy."

Cindy walked toward Kade, shaking her finger. "Do not disrespect the ones that were sent to help you. We work for our Father, and you will show your gratitude by praying with us when we say to."

"I will not pray to *your* God." Kade spat out. "He is not the same God that *I* love."

Suddenly, without warning, Marion's fist smashed into Kade's stomach.

Kade doubled over as he stumbled backwards; the pain shot sharply though his mid-section. He recovered and straightened up. "You will have to kill me before I will pray to *your* God for such nonsense."

This time, it was Buddy that threw the punch at Kade's face. The blow hit him right below his nose on his upper lip.

Kade could feel the warmth from the blood oozing down his chin. But still, he made a vow to himself that he wouldn't coward to these people. He wasn't going to pretend to be someone that he wasn't.

Cindy yelled loudly, "Get him out of here. Take him back. He doesn't get anything to eat until he prays. Only water." She spun around and marched out of the sanctuary.

Marion shoved Kade. "You heard her—go!" He pushed him toward the door.

They took him back to the room he was originally in. Buddy shoved him down onto the bed. "Until you start cooperating it is going to be a long tough road for you. And Cindy won't give in to you. It doesn't bother her to let you go without food."

"Why does that not surprise me," Kade muttered. He'd always had a hard time keeping his mouth shut—even when it was for his own good.

He was sure Marion was about to hit him again, but suddenly he spun toward the door and walked out. Buddy followed him, closing the door. Kade listened as he heard the lock click.

Kade waited until he heard their steps fading down the hallway and then he jumped up and tried the door, knowing it would be locked. He tried the other door in the room. It opened! Kade was quickly disappointed to see it was just a restroom with a single shower, stool, and a sink.

He looked for a window but there weren't any. He went back to the bed and dropped down, face first. Only then did he let the tears come. He'd never been this scared nor this mad before. Surely his father would come to his senses and come back and get him. He quickly wondered if his father would tell his mother where he was. He knew his mom would come as soon as she found out and get him out of this hell hole.

He thought of Cindy and the wild look she had in her eyes. He was sure he'd underestimated her. He couldn't believe anyone could be this evil. *Or could they,* he wondered. He knew one thing: he had to find a way out of here... and soon!

Chapter Fifteen

Monica rushed to the bay window as soon as she heard the car door shut. She was sure it was Karmen, but she was still hopeful that it could be Kade

Disappointed, she watched Karmen as she climbed out of Wayne's car. Monica yelled back at Simon in the kitchen. "It's just Karmen."

Karmen rushed through door. "Oh, Mom, I have something important to tell you." She motioned for her to take a seat on the couch.

Simon entered the room and sat down next to Monica.

"What is it, Karm?" Monica asked. "You look like you have seen a ghost. Is it about Kade?" Her heart sank. She prayed it wasn't more bad news.

"Yeah, it is." She paced nervously in front of the window. "After dad picked me up, we stopped by his house so he could change. I stayed in the car while he went inside. As I was waiting, I remembered that I left my sunglasses in his car the last time I was with him. I didn't see them anywhere so I opened up the glove compartment to see if he'd stuck them in there." She stopped pacing and spun around to glare wide-eyed at her mom. "They weren't in there…but guess what was?"

Monica had no clue what her daughter was getting at. "What? Tell us!"

Karmen reached inside her purse and tossed a cell phone on the coffee table. "Kade's cell phone."

"Are you kidding?" Monica looked at Simon, puzzled. "What did your dad say about it?"

"Umm, I didn't say anything to him about it. I didn't know what to do. I just hid it in my purse." Tears slowly oozed down Karmen's cheek. "I don't know what Daddy knows, but I know he loves Kade."

Monica's jaw dropped as she stared speechlessly at Karmen. Although her words had sunk in, they weren't making any sense to her whatsoever.

She knew Wayne was upset about Kade being gay, but she also knew that Wayne would never put him in harm's way…or would he? "Oh my God, I don't know what to think." She jumped to her feet. "Damn you, Wayne. I will kill you if you have hurt Kade." She stomped her feet like an angry kid. "Where's my cell. I'm calling him and finding out what the hell is going on?"

"Monica, wait," Simon said.

Karmen interrupted. "You can't, Mom. Dad will be furious that I took it out of the glove compartment."

Monica spun and stared at Karmen. "Dad will be furious," she mocked. "Are you kidding me, Karm? Your brother is missing and could be in danger, and your father has something to do with it—and you're worried about your father being mad?"

"I'm sorry, Mom. It does sound silly, I guess."

147

"Shouldn't we think this through before we jump to conclusions?" Simon stood and wrapped his arm around Monica's shoulders.

"What do you think?" She turned toward Simon. "Why else would he have Kade's phone? He has to know where Kade is." Monica let the tears flow. "That bastard! What has he done?"

Simon rubbed Monica's back. "Come on, Monica. You have to calm down." Simon snatched Kade's cell phone off the table. "I know—why don't we check his phone and see when he used it last."

"Of course," Monica nodded. "That would be smart."

Simon searched through Kade's phone history as Monica and Karmen gazed over his shoulder.

Monica instantly spotted where Kade had returned her call yesterday. That was the last phone conversation he'd had. There were no text messages going out, either, except to Luke from earlier times.

Simon set the phone back on the table. "Well, at least we know Kade didn't have his phone after he got off work. So I think something had to have happened after he left work."

"I have to call Wayne. I can't wait any longer." Monica glanced from Karmen to Simon.

"Should you call the police first?" Simon asked.

Karmen quickly chimed in. "No, Mom, please. Don't call the police yet. Please call dad first and see what he says," She was near tears. "Maybe Kade is okay."

Monica reluctantly agreed. "Okay, I will let him explain first. But he better have an answer for me, or I am calling the police."

Monica took a deep breath, called Wayne's cell phone, and walked toward the window as she waited for him to answer.

After several rings he answered, "Hello."

Monica's voice quivered as she spoke, "Wayne, where is our son?" She wasn't going to beat around the bush; she didn't have time for his games.

"What are you talking about, Monica?" Wayne stuttered. "You mean he still hasn't come home yet?"

"Don't play with me, Wayne. I know you know where he is! Karm found his cell phone in your glove compartment."

There was a long pause before he spoke again. "I don't know what you are talking about. I didn't have his cell phone, and I have no clue where Kade is."

"Are you calling your daughter a liar?"

"I'm just saying I don't know what you're talking about, Monica. And frankly, I don't have time for this right now."

"Damn you, Wayne. Don't screw with me. If you don't tell me where our son is, I *am* calling the police."

"Monica, you are losing your mind. I don't know anything—so you do whatever you want." He paused. "Maybe Karmen has had his phone. Maybe she knows something. I just know she didn't get it out of my glove compartment."

"So help me, Wayne. If you have hurt Kade in any way—I will make you pay dearly. Bastard, I hate you." She tossed her phone on the couch. She turned to Karmen, "Your dear sweet father thinks you are lying. He said you didn't get the cell phone out of his glove compartment and that maybe you have had it and know something."

Karmen's eyes widened. "Omigod! You don't believe that, do you, Mom?"

"Of course not, sweetie. Your dad is hiding something, and I'm going to find out what it is right now." Monica grabbed Simon's hand. "I hate to ask you to do this, but would you mind driving me down to the police station?"

She held out her trembling hand. "I am shaking. I don't think I am able to drive."

"You don't have to ask, Monica. You know I will." He glanced around the room. "Grab what you need and let's go. You better take Kade's phone—they will likely want to see it."

"Can I go?" Karmen asked.

"It's okay with me if your mom doesn't mind." Simon nodded toward Monica.

"You can go but you might not like what I have to say about your dad." Monica snatched her purse off the kitchen table.

"I don't mind. Not now, anyway—after dad called me a liar." Her eyes clouded over.

Monica felt her pain. *How sad she must be,* she thought. She quickly hugged her daughter. "I am so sorry, sweetie. Your father is not who we thought he was. I know how disappointed you must be." She held her at arm's length. "But I love you with all of my heart, so don't ever forget that! Right now, we have to find your brother before it's too late." She shoved Karmen toward the door while her own words echoed in her head, *'before it's too late.'*

***

Tuesday, July 15, 6:30 a.m.

Kade woke up to the clicking of the door being unlocked. He didn't remember falling asleep. He recalled crying and praying but couldn't recall when he fell asleep. His stomach roared. The hunger was settling in and, as much as he hated to do it, he didn't want to starve to death either. He decided he would pretend to pray to Cindy's God so he could get some food.

Buddy and Marion entered the room, looking rested and cleaned up.

Marion spoke first, "Are you ready to start asking God to forgive you for your sins?"

Buddy added rudely, "Or would you prefer no breakfast too?"

Kade bit down on his lower lip. "I will pray now," he said, not sounding the least bit sincere.

Marion's eyes widened. "Good. Cindy will be waiting for us." He glanced at Buddy. "Grab him some clothes. He must shower before we take him down there.

Buddy disappeared through the door and returned within a few minutes. He handed Kade a long black robe, black boxer shorts, and some black slippers. "You will be wearing this for now on—until God has forgiven you." He nodded to the restroom door. "Hurry and shower. There is a toothbrush is in the medicine cabinet. We will be back in ten minutes. Be ready. Cindy does not fancy to late arrivals." He glanced at his watch and followed Marion out the door.

Kade glanced down at his new attire and rolled his eyes. He couldn't believe this. But he was hungry and until he could find a way to get out of here, he'd have to pretend to believe their garbage.

When Buddy and Marion returned, Kade was ready to play their little game. He followed them quietly to the sanctuary. Shortly after they had kneeled at the pew, Cindy entered the room and took the same position at the podium. She bent her head and seemed to be saying a silent prayer. She suddenly glanced up at Kade, "I'm glad you have come to your senses. Now we need to pray, and God will start his forgiveness process. But you must know that God will know if you are being sincere. You do understand that, Kade, don't you?"

"Yes," he muttered. All he could think about was food. He could care less about all this nonsense. He would not let her accusations bother him. He would pretend, he told himself—just like he did in his high school theatre class.

"Bow your heads," Cindy hissed. "Father, we have brought a sinner to you today. He has realized that he has been leading a sinful lifestyle and following acts of Satan. He is here today to confess his sins to you and ask for your forgiveness." She raised her head, "Kade, tell our Father about your sins."

Kade tried to swallow the lump in his throat. He wasn't expecting to have to talk and it had caught him off guard. He didn't know if he could pull this off without Cindy knowing he wasn't being sincere. This was a real test of his acting skills.

"Dear Father," he started, "I have been sinning because I am attracted to men rather than women. I should be punished for the way I feel." Kade knew he sounded sarcastic on his last comment and hoped Cindy didn't pick up on it. He continued to ramble on words that he thought Cindy would want to hear. A few times he almost laughed at how silly he sounded.

Finally, an hour later after listening to Cindy preach, she dismissed him to go back to his room to eat breakfast. He'd never been so relieve in his life.

It wasn't until Marion and Buddy had dropped off a tray and left the room that he bowed his head and prayed to *his* God. "Please, God, let my mom find me. I can't do this!"

152

Chapter Sixteen

Later:

Monica was furious. She paced the parking lot, irritated as hell. She spent the whole evening at the police station the night before, and Sgt. Finch had promised they would question Wayne first thing this morning.

She had Simon bring her to the station at ten this morning, giving them plenty of time to interrogate Wayne. Now an hour later she didn't know anything more than she did when she arrived.

Sgt. Finch had questioned Wayne but was convinced that he didn't know anything. Monica pleaded with the Sergeant to question Wayne further, but Sgt. Finch said he didn't have any grounds to keep on grilling him.

Monica had asked to speak to someone higher up and another officer confirmed what Sgt. Finch had told her. They said that even the cell phone wasn't enough proof because Karmen had retrieved it instead of leaving it in the glove compartment. The Sergeant claimed they had no proof that it was ever in the glove compartment. He even suggested that maybe Karmen knew Kade's whereabouts.

Monica had stormed out of the station, fuming. How could they not connect the dots and see that Wayne was obviously involved in Kade's disappearance?

She pretended to kick the car door. "Damn it! What am I supposed to do now? Wayne knows where Kade is. I know he does."

"I'm thinking," Simon rested his hands on his hips. After a few silent moments he continued, "We need to get the media involved. I have a friend that works for Fox4 news. I could give her a call if you want."

"That's brilliant." Monica kissed him on the cheek. "You are so smart.

"Maybe, if the media is involved, it will put a little pressure on the police. Why don't I drive you back to the house to get your car and you go talk to the newspaper while I try to get a hold of Dana."

"Sounds like a plan. I will get Karmen to go with me. Be sure to tell Dana about Wayne and what we suspect."

"Oh, don't worry. I will."

Monica jumped in the car and fastened her seat belt. She was so thankful she had Simon to help her through this; she'd be lost without him. What an awesome idea. Maybe the media could pressure Wayne into telling the truth if the police wouldn't do anything. She was determined to find her son...one way or another.

***

Later: 5:00 p.m.

Monica parked her car down the street from Wayne's house. She didn't want to draw any attention to their scheme. The newscast was supposed to meet them at

5:15p.m. in front of his house to do a live interview. Monica was sure he'd be home from work by five. She could hardly wait to see his face when they try to interview him. The news reporter had already been informed on Wayne's alleged involvement.

She waited until she saw Simon parking behind her and then glanced at Karmen. "Are you sure you're okay with this?"

"I don't really like the way we are doing this without daddy knowing. But if it is our only chance to find Kade then I guess we don't have any choice."

"I know you love your father, Karm. And I'm sorry it had to come this, but I really believe he knows where your brother is."

"I know. I do too. It just makes me really sad to think he is in on this."

"I know, honey." Monica spotted Wayne pulling up in his driveway and rushing inside his house. She was glad the news people hadn't arrived yet.

Simon tapped on the window. "You getting out?"

"Come on," she told Karmen. She climbed out of the car, and they all huddled together out of any view of Wayne's house.

A few minutes later, the news van showed up and a pretty blond woman climbed out carrying a microphone. The camera men were close behind her.

Simon quickly approached Dana and introduced her to Monica and Karmen.

Dana quickly went over the details with Monica and Karmen and motioned for the camera men that she was ready. She had Monica tell the story from the time of Kade's disappearance. She also had Monica describe him and the accomplishments he earned in high school. She finished by stating that Kade is gay and that his father would not accept it.

Then Dana turned her attention to Karmen and asked her about the cell phone she'd found in Wayne's glove compartment.

Karmen confirmed that she found Kade's cell phone in her dad's car the night before.

Monica wasn't aware that Wayne had come out on his porch. Suddenly, he was standing there in his shorts and t-shirt, rubbing his head as if in disbelief. "What is going on?" he shouted across the yard.

"Mr. Myers, we were just discussing with your wife and daughter about your son's disappearance. They seem to believe you might know where he is."

"I don't know where he is!"

"Is it true that you were upset to find out that your son was gay?"

"Maybe I am. But that doesn't mean I know where he is."

"Is it true that your daughter found Kade's cell phone in your glove compartment?"

Monica could tell Wayne was totally caught off guard by the question. He glanced toward Karmen and seemed to be struggling how to answer.

"I didn't put it there."

"Are you implying that your daughter is making this up?" Dana asked.

Wayne glanced toward Karmen, and Monica knew in that instant that he did love Karmen even if he had no feelings toward his son any more.

Wayne shrugged nervously. "*I* said I didn't put it there. If she found it there, I don't know how it could have possibly gotten there."

"That doesn't make sense, Mr. Myers. Are you implying you never saw Kade the day he disappeared?"

Wayne was scrambling for words now. "I don't remember, but I don't think so."

"How can you *not* remember if you saw your son?" Dana asked.

"Because it is confidential—that's why?"

"You have a worried mother and sister over there." Dana nodded toward Monica and Karmen. "If there is something you know about Kade's whereabouts, then shouldn't they be informed?"

Wayne's voice grew loud, "My son asked me for help because he didn't want to be gay any longer. So I helped him like any other father would do." He threw his hands up in the air. "Now get the hell off my property before I call the police." He spun on his heels and marched into his house, slamming the door behind him.

Monica's jaw dropped. "Omigod," she whispered. "What has he done to *my* son?"

***

Kade had had enough—he'd done everything the crazy lady had told him to. He pretended to be sincere and pray to her God. He'd muttered tons of words that he didn't mean. But now she'd gone too far.

All day he cooperated and was rewarded with praise and food.

But he didn't deserve this. "I'm not doing it," he told Cindy.

"God will not forgive you unless you can feel pain. You have caused our Father great pain. Now you must feel pain in order to prove you will be forgiven."

"I don't care what you say," Kade mouthed. "I am not letting them wax the hair off my legs and chest. That is just nuts." He shook his head. "I have apologized to your God and that's it. I'm done. I'm not playing this stupid little charade of yours anymore."

Suddenly Marion and Buddy grabbed his arms. He tried to pull away from them, but they were too strong.

Cindy closed her eyes and held up her hands. "Forgive him, Father. He doesn't know what he is talking about. We will show him and lead him in the right direction for you, Father." She opened her eyes and nodded toward Marion and Buddy. "Make him understand. Tie him up if you have to—just get it though his head that he will do what I tell him to, whether he likes it or not." Her eyes narrowed as she moved toward Kade. She stopped directly in front of him. "Let me tell you what—if you don't change that attitude of yours, you will go to bed hungry many of nights and you will experience a lot of agony. My boys have no problem inflicting pain on those that do not obey the Lord's commandments." She stuck her face within a couple of inches of Kade's. "Do you understand me?"

Kade wanted nothing more than to spit in her face. Unfortunately, it wasn't possible because his arms were already sore from the tight hold that Marion and Buddy had on him. He knew she wasn't bluffing and one little negative move from him would probably result in a lot of pain. As stubborn as he was, he knew that he'd be foolish not to agree with her. He nodded but couldn't help but roll his eyes as soon as she turned her back.

"Get him out of here," she shouted as she marched toward the door. "Tie him up and wax all the hair off of his legs and chest. He is *not* to have any dinner either."

"Yes, Ma'am," Marion and Buddy said, simultaneously.

They jerked Kade out of the room.

Kade didn't try to resist. He knew it would be a lost cause. As much as he tried to be strong and hold back the tears, he felt one of them get away and roll down his cheek.

He'd never met anyone in his life like Cindy. Her thinking was so bizarre. *What would removing the hair on him prove anyway?*

Marion and Buddy led him to an empty room at the end of the hallway. The room was small and hot. There was a wide table the length of the room in the center. There was a smaller stand next to it with all kinds of supplies like tape, cotton, and rope. There was a small kettle that Kade assumed was holding the hot wax. The room almost felt like some kind of operating room. *The only thing missing is a knife,* he thought, *but I wouldn't be surprised if one wasn't hidden somewhere.*

Kade climbed upon the table like he was instructed to do and laid flat on his back. He closed his eyes. He knew he couldn't trust these people and wouldn't be safe as long as he was here. He squeezed his eyes shut to avoid the tears from falling. He wondered how much worse this nightmare would get before it came to an end. Or if it would ever come to an end?

Chapter Seventeen

Later: 8:45p.m.

Monica leaned forward and grasped the edge of her chair as she tried to digest Sgt. Finch words: Wayne couldn't be found. *Omigod,* she thought, *this couldn't be happening.*

The last few hours had been a nightmare. After Dana and her crew had left Wayne's house, Monica had banged on his door, demanding him to tell her where Kade was. Wayne hadn't responded. Even Karmen had begged her dad to open the door, but he wouldn't do it.

An hour later, Simon suggested they go back to the police station. By this time, other media reporters had caught air of Dana's report and had shown up at Wayne's house. They all wanted live interviews from Monica.

Monica gladly gave them each a full report, hoping to get as much attention to Kade's case as possible. If Wayne wouldn't talk, at least she could rat him out to everyone and let them know the scumbag that he was.

Many of the reporters were still hanging around Wayne's house when she left. She'd been in a hurry to get to the police station to see what Sgt. Finch had planned for Wayne now.

The sergeant had her wait out in the lobby for over an hour while he got his unit together. He'd send them out with orders to bring Wayne in for more questioning.

She should have known by the way Sgt. Finch called them into his office that something was wrong. He wasn't acting as confident as he'd been earlier—almost as if something didn't go as he had planned.

Finally, Monica spoke, "What do you mean they can't find him?"

Simon grabbed Monica's hand and squeezed it, while Karmen stood and walked toward the back of the room.

Sgt. Finch cleared his throat, "Apparently his car is missing too."

"But how could he have gotten away with all of the reporters surrounding the house?" Monica asked.

"Yeah," Simon agreed. "They didn't look like they were leaving anytime soon. I figured they would hang around until morning and wait for him to come out."

"It's possible there were some reporters still there when he made his escape. We just need to find the right people that know something. My men are on top of this now as we speak."

A small sob escaped from Karmen in the back of the room and Monica rushed to console her.

Monica wrapped her arms around her and pulled her close. "You okay?"

"I just want all of this to stop!" Karmen's tear spilled down her blushed cheeks. "Where is my brother? And what has my daddy done? I love them both so much."

161

Simon was fast to the rescue. "Hey, Karm. Why don't we go down to the vending machines and get a soda? You probably could use a break from all of this."

Monica mouthed thank you silently to Simon and then lifted Karmen's chin up. "Simon's right. You don't need to be in here anyway. This is too hard for you. Take a break. I will be out shortly."

Karmen didn't argue; she followed Simon out of the room.

Monica waited until the door had shut and then turned her attention back to Sgt. Finch. "Okay, now what?"

He glanced at his watch. "Well, it's going on nine and there's not really much else we can do until we locate your ex-husband."

Monica glanced nervously down at her own watch. She wished it wasn't so late. "What if Wayne can't be found?"

"I know you're upset, Monica. Believe me, I don't blame you. But we are doing all we can do at this time." Sgt. Finch walked over to his door and opened it. "Why don't you go home and get some rest, and I will contact you as soon as we find Mr. Myers."

Monica walked toward the door. She knew Sgt. Finch's gesture was a hint for her to leave now. "And you will call me as soon as they find him?"

"I will," he promised.

"Is there anything I should be doing?" She felt so helpless.

"You need to rest, Monica. If your ex has anything to do with your son's disappearance, we *will* find out what it is. I'd like to hope that he wouldn't put his own son in harm. And who knows, he may be bluffing, too. He might not really know where Kade is." He walked Monica out into the hallway. "We will just have to wait and see what he has to say. But I will call you if I hear anything."

Monica wanted to say more but didn't. "Okay, thanks."

She walked to the lobby where Simon and Karmen were waiting. "I guess we go home and wait," she told them.

"I need to eat something." Karmen rubbed her hand over her stomach. "I don't feel so good."

"Why don't I take Karm to get something to eat and I will meet you at your house," Simon offered.

"That sounds good. I need to think anyway." Monica unlocked her car door.

"We will bring you something back to eat. What are you hungry for?"

"It doesn't matter. I'm not that hungry." She climbed into her car. "I'll see you shortly." She slammed the door shut.

She waited until she was out of the parking lot before she let the tears fall. She was overwhelmed with fear.

She decided to drive back by Wayne's house to see if he'd come home yet. She couldn't imagine how he was involved in Kade's disappearance, but she was certain that he was.

Monica was glad the police were finally taking this a little bit more serious now that it had hit the news. Surely, they would find Kade now.

She needed more than anything to see her son. She had to believe that he was okay and would be home soon. She had to have faith or she would fall apart if she let her mind think any differently.

Kade turned sideways on the bed and wept like a five year old child. He didn't care either—at least he hadn't shed a tear during the waxing. It had hurt like hell but he was bound and determined not to let Marion and Buddy think they were getting the best of him. Even the gay jokes hadn't made him crack.

But now that he was alone back in the solitary room, he sobbed. The waxing not only hurt but was humiliating. Buddy would make comments such as: 'Since you like guys so much we will shave your legs and chest and then you will look more like a girl.' Then Marion would chuckle which would only encourage Buddy to make more jokes.

Kade felt broken now. He'd never felt so isolated and alone before. He couldn't believe that people could actually hate him just because of his sexuality. They didn't even know him.

He opened his eyes and glanced to the ceiling. "It's not fair, God," he muttered. "I didn't ask to be this way." He wiped at his nose. "Why? Why me, God?"

Kade didn't like to question God. He knew that he had his reasons for everything he had done. But he was pissed. "Damn it, God!" He smashed his fist against the bed. "Why couldn't I just be normal?"

Suddenly, he felt horrible for his thoughts. "I'm sorry, God." He instantly felt remorse for pitying himself. There were far worse things in life and he knew it. He should be grateful for all that God had done for him and the talents that he'd been blessed with.

He was just angry at the haters. The people that wouldn't accept him for who he was and the ones that thought they had the right to judge him. He found it unbelievable how some of them could judge others like they did and call themselves Christians. 'We live by the bible,' they would say while shaking their fingers at homosexuals.

Kade wish he could shout back at them, 'No, you don't, either.' But he'd never lower himself to their standards. He knew God would be the one to judge them in the end and that it wasn't his job to do so.

He thought of his father and his heart grew heavy. He was mostly sad that his father could hate him so much to lock him in such a horrid place like this. He didn't understand how a father could do this to his own son.

Kade had loved his dad so much—*but not anymore*. He would never forgive him for this—*ever*. He hated him. It was the first time Kade had admitted such thoughts and it felt great. "I hate you, Dad." He was proud that he could say it out loud without feeling guilty. He raised his voice even louder, "I hate you for everything you stand for. I hate you for the way you think and for the way you have treated me." He jumped to his feet and shouted at the door. "I will never forgive you for bringing me to this hell hole. I hate these people here and everything they are trying to prove." He banged his fists against the door. "I hate it here. I want to go home. You people are idiots!"

He waited silently.

Kade wasn't sure what he was expecting. He thought maybe Marion and Buddy would come and try to make him shut up. He was ready for them. He was determined to fight his way out. But they didn't come. Kade didn't even hear footsteps. It was as if they weren't even around.

He fell back on the bed and sobbed more. He didn't know how long he cried before he finally drifted to sleep.

***

Monica drove slowly by Wayne's house. The lights were off inside, and Wayne's car was nowhere in sight. The reporters had all gone home and the street was deserted.

Monica debated what to do. She circled back around the block as her mind raced. She was sure Wayne knew where Kade was and couldn't wait any longer.

She pulled up to the curb a block away from Wayne's house. She shifted the car in park. Monica knew what she had to do even though she risked getting in trouble for it. She grabbed the flashlight out of her glove compartment and swung the car door open.

She glanced around the area before climbing out of the car. She quickly jogged up the block and around to the back of the house. Wayne had always insisted on keeping a spare key at the back door and she hoped he hadn't changed his theory.

She turned the flashlight toward the back porch. "Bingo," she whispered. A brown flower pot set right on the top stair. She quickly lifted it up and spotted a silver key chain with a single key dangling from it. *Too easy,* she thought.

She quickly inserted the key and slipped inside the house.

Monica flicked the flashlight around the kitchen and moved quietly into the hallway. It didn't take but a few moments to locate Wayne's bedroom. She spotted the light switch but thought it too risky to flip it on. Instead, she used the flashlight to search the dressers. Not finding anything out of the ordinary, she returned to the hallway to search the other rooms.

The only thing that caught her eye was the women's house slippers in the main bathroom. A month ago, she might have been jealous, but now she only pitied the woman that they belong to.

She scratched her head. "Okay, Wayne, give me something to go on here." She ventured back into the computer room. She didn't know why she didn't think of his computer in the first place. He was so predictable; she was sure he hadn't thought to change his passwords, either.

Sure enough, she typed his old password and easily booted up the computer. She went straight to his email account. She typed his middle name and birthday in again and just like that she was in his email account.

She laughed. "You were never as sneaky as you thought you were," she mumbled.

She scrolled through his email, not quite sure what she was searching for.

Suddenly her eyes settled on one particular headline and she stared blankly at the words. Her heart raced as she read it, 'Turning Gays Straight.' She stared in disbelief.

Monica suddenly glanced toward the window. She'd heard a car door slam. *Could it be Wayne?* She glanced back at the email. She didn't care at this point. She had to know the truth.

She quickly clicked on the email to open it. She heard a key in the front door. "Oh, crap!" she whispered. "I'm busted!"

Chapter Eighteen

Monica's whole body shook with fear but she didn't move away from the computer. She heard Wayne go from the front room into the kitchen; the light flipped on.

She scanned the computer screen. She couldn't believe the words she'd quickly skimmed over. A lady named Cindy Walker was requesting $10,000 up front for some services that Wayne was asking for. She didn't have time to digest what it all meant.

She could hear Wayne opening drawers in the kitchen and figured he must be getting something to eat. She found the website address and quickly memorized it. She exited out of the email and quickly put the computer back to sleep.

She prayed that Wayne didn't decide to come into the computer room next. She ducked into the open closet just in case he did.

After several long moments, she heard him go into his bedroom. She sighed with relief. A few minutes later, she heard the shower running and knew this would be her only chance to escape.

She scurried toward the door and down the hallway. She darted into the kitchen and quietly slipped out the back door. She pulled the door shut and hurriedly slipped the key under the flower pot. It wasn't until then that she realized she'd left the flashlight sitting on the desk.

"Damn," she muttered under her breath. She debated whether or not to go back in to get it. She decided she couldn't take that chance.

She jogged to her car, thankful that she'd parked a ways from his house. She was certain he would see the flashlight on his desk, but she wasn't sure if he'd figure out that it belonged to her. In the past, he would always tease her for keeping a flashlight in her purse. However, this one was cheap and far different from the pocket size one that he'd recognized.

At this point she really didn't care if he figured out that it was hers. He wouldn't be able to prove it—and besides he should be more concerned about saving his own ass right now.

She drove anxiously away from Wayne's house as the horrifying words she'd read flashed through her head. It was some kind of place that promised they could turn any homosexual straight. It had labeled *gays* as the 'devil's children'.

Monica suddenly felt nauseous. There was no doubt in her mind that Wayne had taken Kade to some insane place. "Dear God, please let my son be all right," she said out loud. She couldn't imagine what Kade could be going through or what kind of nonsense they could be filling his head with.

She pressed on the gas pedal. She had to get home and pull up this website to see where this crazy place was. She wasn't even going to bother telling the police what she found out; they'd have to go through their step-by-step procedures...it would take way too long.

Then they'd want to know how she came upon this information. She'd probably get in trouble for breaking into Wayne's house and then she wouldn't be able to help Kade.

She continued to ride in silence, as she deliberated what to do. She wanted to go find Kade herself, but she wasn't sure if Simon would go along with her plan.

Finally, she reached her house. She snatched her purse and jumped out of the car. She was suddenly surrounded by three reporters. She had no clue where they had all come from.

"Mrs. Myers, can you tell us if your son has been found yet?" the pretty young redhead asked.

Before she could respond, an elderly man chimed in, "Did they locate your ex-husband yet?"

The other plump, balding gentleman pushed his microphone in front of Monica. "Would you like to make a statement? The viewers are concerned about your son."

Monica held up her hand. "I'm sorry to say that Kade hasn't been found yet. And, yes, Wayne Myers's car *is* at his house, and I *do* believe he knows where our son is."

The reporters thanked her and headed for their cars. She knew exactly where they were going.

Simon was sitting on the couch but immediately jumped to his feet. "Where have you been? I've been worried sick about you. It's almost midnight."

"I'm sorry." Monica rushed passed him to the computer room. "I think I know where Kade is." She pushed the power button on her computer. "I haven't had time to call you."

"That's okay .You have a ton of calls on your answering machine. Crystal is worried sick about you. I explained the situation to her, and she wants you to call her when you get a chance.

170

Monica nodded. "I should have thought to call her sooner."

"And all the reporters' calls," Simon continued, "I just let the machine take the messages. I wasn't dealing with them without you." He sighed.

"Boy, they sure are assertive. Three of them caught me outside just now." Monica tapped her fingernails against the desk as she waited for the computer to boot.

"Well, where do you think Kade could be?" Simon asked.

"I'm not positive. I will have to show you." Monica clicked on the Internet and typed in the webpage. "I snuck into Wayne's house and got on his computer."

"You didn't!"

"I did." She glanced up to see the reaction on Simon's face—he was shocked. "I had to. I knew he knew something!"

The website loaded and Monica pointed to the screen. "I think Wayne might have taken Kade here."

They both viewed the webpage in silence, reading over all of the materials.

"You have got to be kidding me!" Simon shook his head. "I have never heard of such a place."

"I know," Monica agreed. "Poor Kade." She scribbled down the address. She guessed it was over an hour drive. "Where's Karm?"

"She couldn't stay awake. She went on to bed."

"That's okay. It's probably best she didn't go."

Simon looked puzzled. "What do you have planned?"

"I'm going to find my son!" She stood and snatched her keys.

"You're not calling the police first?"

"Are you kidding? Kade could be dead by the time they got around to looking for him."

"Are you crazy? You can't go get him! It's way too dangerous."

"There's nothing you can say, Simon that is going to change my mind. My son could be in great danger and I'm going to help him if I have to do it myself." She hurried into the living room to gather her purse.

Simon shrugged and followed her into the living room. "Well, then I'm going with you."

She spun around to face him. "No way! You stay here with Karm. I will be fine."

Simon grabbed Monica's shoulder. "Listen here, young lady. There's nothing you can say to keep me from going with you." He smiled. "Besides, I have a plan. I will call Dana and have her meet us there with the crew. Surely, nothing can go wrong if reporters are all around."

"Wow, that's a great idea." She quickly kissed him on the cheek. "Thanks, Simon, for everything."

"Of course." He grabbed her hand as they walked toward the door. "We will call the police when we get almost there. That way it won't look like we did something without them knowing about it."

"Perfect." She caught sight of a reporter climbing out of his car as soon as he spotted them. "What about them?"

"Let's try to ditch them. Don't answer anything if they ask." Simon bowed his head to the ground and continued to walk. "What about Karmen?"

"She'll be fine. If she wakes up, she'll call me. But I doubt if she'll be up until morning." She hurried to her car, ignoring the reporter. She quickly jumped behind the wheel. "And by then, maybe Kade will be home." She could only hope anyway.

"We can take my car if you want."

"No, I'm fine." She waited for Simon to pull his door shut. "I just want to get there as fast as we can." She slammed the car in drive and pulled away from the curb.

"Let's just make sure we get there alive, or we would have gone through all of this work for nothing."

Monica laughed, "I promise I will watch my speed, Mr. Smarty-pants." She had a feeling, though; the next hour was going to be the longest hour of her life.

***

Kade suddenly woke. *Where is the music coming from?* He sat up and listened. "Leave me alone," he shouted. It was some sort of song about asking the Lord to forgive you for your sins, or you would burn in Hell. The chorus kept repeating over and over. Kade could tell it wasn't a professional song—it sounded more like a group of amateurs singing while someone else recorded it.

Kade put his hands over his ears. It was a horrible song. *How could people be so cruel*, he wondered.

His stomach ached with hunger, and his lips were dry. He wondered what time it was and how long he'd been asleep. It was hard to tell anything without any windows in the room.

He went into the bathroom and shut the door, but the song still continued. He glanced around to see where the sound was coming from and spotted a speaker behind the trash can.

Kade moaned—if anything would drive him insane, it would be that song.

He splashed cold water on his face and then stuck his face down and guzzled water from the faucet. It didn't stop the hunger pains, but at least it was wet and cold.

He froze. He thought he heard the lock click in the other room. He opened the bathroom door and was surprised to see Buddy standing in the center of the room with a bible.

"It's time for prayer," he stated.

"What?" Kade asked. "What time is it?"

"It's 1:30 in the morning. I am on prayer duty tonight with you. You will have to pray around the clock and it's still not guaranteed that our Father will forgive you."

Kade suddenly wondered if he could overpower this guy. He wasn't all that tall, but he had some weight on him that could give him more strength.

Kade didn't have to wonder for long. It was as if Buddy had read his mind.

"Don't even think about getting cute with me. I came prepared." He flashed a pistol sticking out of the pocket of his jeans. "Now get moving."

Kade slowly walked into the hallway and waited for Buddy to pull the door shut. He couldn't believe they were going to pray again at this time of night. The song kept playing and was filling his head. He almost had the chorus memorized and not by choice either. He wondered if this was the way people were brainwashed.

Kade thought if he was here too long, maybe they could possibly brainwash him and make him think he was an evil person.

No, he couldn't let himself think that way. He knew his faith would keep him true to himself and the way God intended him to be. He wasn't going to change for any of the haters in this world who think they know everything about being different.

He followed Buddy to the pew and bowed his head. Kade pretended to be praying as Buddy's words went in one ear and out the other while his own thoughts occupied his time.

Kade didn't understand why it was so hard for people to accept homosexuals. They could take one sentence in the bible and blow it up into what they interpret it to mean. They didn't realize that the bible was written before they even knew homosexuals existed. He also didn't understand how some Christians could pursue one part of the bible but ignore the rest of the bible; it didn't make sense.

What really irritated him the most were the people that thought they could convince homosexuals to believe that they *choose to be gay. How could anyone know that unless they were actually gay?*

He knew homosexuals had been trying to voice their opinion for years and let people know that they didn't choose to be gay. But a lot of society still wanted to believe that they were all lying.

Kade thought the root of the problem went even deeper than that. He believed even if there was proof that homosexuals didn't choose to be gay, that it still wouldn't matter to the haters. They would continue to discriminate, regardless. They would find one reason after another to hate homosexuality.

He firmly believed that prejudice would continue until the youth was educated differently. There had to be some major changes in society in order for gays to start being viewed differently. For one thing, the jokes have to stop. As long as joking about gays continue, it will be passed down to our youth and the discrimination will remain.

Buddy interrupted his thoughts. "Speak to our Father and tell him how sorry you are for how you have been behaving. Ask our Lord to help you stay clear from Satan."

Kade let words flow out of his mouth that he wasn't even aware he was saying. He needed food, and he knew he had to let these nuts think he was sorry for the way he was. He glanced toward Buddy—his eyes were closed, so he assumed he was doing a good job at bullshitting.

Kade thought of John. It seemed like forever since his death now. He wondered how he would have handled a place like this. Kade's eyes watered. He missed his friend—he didn't deserve to die at such a young age. If only John would have believed in himself—but he'd figured if no one else loved him for who he really was, how could he love himself?

Kade had read tons of stories similar to John's. There were so many teens and young adults that had killed themselves because society had treated them like freaks.

Suddenly, Kade didn't care anymore about food or this ridiculous place. He spoke loudly, "John, if you can hear me…if it is the last thing I do, I am going to help other homosexuals from feeling the way you did. I am going to show them that their life is worth something. I do not want anyone to ever be as unhappy as you were! No one deserves to be treated the way you were or the way I am being treated now."

"Shut up now before I make you shut up," Buddy shouted at him.

Kade opened his eyes and stared at Buddy. He could tell he was furious. He face was flushed and he was gritting his teeth together.

But once again, Kade was in his 'I don't care mode.' He glared at Buddy. "Go to hell. I'm leaving this damn place right now. Shoot me if you want." He stood and ripped off the horrible black robe that they had made him wear over his work clothes.

Kade stepped backwards as Buddy slowly moved toward him—rage was written all over his face as he pulled the pistol out of his jeans.

Suddenly, Kade was second guessing the scenario he'd just created. But he knew it was too late!

Chapter Nineteen

Wednesday July 16, 2008, 2:10 a.m.

Monica double checked the address again with the numbers on the front of the huge brick building. They matched. She would have thought the building to be deserted if it wasn't for the single light shining through the window and the little blue Ford Focus parked in the parking lot.

It was definitely an older building and located on the worst side of the city. The further she'd driven into the neighborhood, the worse the buildings became. Most of them were boarded up.

She killed the ignition and stared ahead at the dreary building. "Omigod!" She glanced at Simon. "Do you think Kade could be in there?"

"Any other time I would say I hope not, but under these circumstances, I pray that he is."

Monica glanced up and down the deserted street. Besides the Focus, there wasn't a car in sight—not even a parked one. "What should we do now?" The building gave her an eerie feeling. She was starting to wish the police were with them.

"We need to wait for Dana and her crew. When they get here, I will go knock on the door before the police get here." He glanced at his watch. "I'm not sure how much the police will be able to do at this point. I'm sure they will have to have a warrant. So if Kade is in there, maybe all the reporters being here will scare whoever into letting him go."

"That sounds like a good plan." She wiped at the sweat forming on her brows. "I'm really nervous." She glanced in the rear view mirror. "If Dana's not here soon, I won't be able to wait. I have to know if Kade is in there and if he is okay."

Simon rubbed his hand across Monica's hand. "I know how you must feel, but we would be foolish to do anything before the reporters get here. Besides, I'm going to the doo—not you."

Monica rolled her eyes. "Ha! Over my dead body you are. I am going up there. Believe me—you're not going to be able to stop me."

Simon smiled. "The more I know you—the more I know not to argue with you when your mind is made up." He squeezed her hand. "But I am going with you and over my dead body will you be able to stop me."

She had to smile although her mind-set was far from happiness. "Okay, I agree."

Suddenly she spotted headlights rounding the corner. Her adrenaline began to race—she was certain that it was Dana.

Monica and Simon climbed out of the car and waited for the van to pull up next to them.

Dana climbed out of the passenger's side while three other men crawled out from the back. They immediately started pulling cameras and equipment out of the van.

"I apologize for being late. I got everyone together as quick as I could." She rolled her eyes. "Unfortunately, it leaked out where we were headed. So I imagine before long we will have company."

"That's okay. We haven't been waiting too long," Simon said. "We had to make a stop ourselves to get gas."

Although Monica was following the conversation between Dana and Simon, her eyes were glued to the building. Her heart was racing. She needed to get inside. She had to know if her son was okay.

She grabbed her keys out of the car and softly shut the door as not to alarm anyone inside the building. "I'm anxious. Can we go now?"

"The police will be here soon." Dana smiled. "But you know I don't have a problem with you guys going on up to the door. I love a good story. And it's rare that we beat the cops to the scene." She glanced at her crew and back to Simon and Monica. "Do you think it is safe?"

"We will find out soon." Monica started toward the building. "Come on, Simon."

Suddenly, a loud bang went off and Monica screamed. "What was that?"

"That scared the crap out of me," Dana said.

"It sounded like a gun." Simon slid up next to Monica. "Maybe we should wait for the police."

Monica's body trembled as her words were rushed, "Are you kidding? Omigod! What if Kade is hurt?" She staggered slightly.

Simon grabbed her arm. "Monica, are you okay? You look like you're going to pass out."

Monica quickly rubbed her fingers around her temples. Her head hurt like hell, but she didn't have time to worry about that now. "I'm fine. Let's just go."

Dana jogged up next to Simon. "Here take this in case you need it." She slid a small black pistol in his hand. "I didn't give it to you though." She winked and scrambled back to her crew.

Monica and Simon sprinted up to the door of the building.

Monica didn't even bother to knock before quickly twisting the doorknob. "Damn it!" She wasn't surprised that it was locked; just disappointed.

Simon banged on the door and they waited.

After several moments, Monica grew impatient. She spotted more headlights pulling up, but still no sirens. She had to get to her son. "Open this damn door," she screamed. "Let us in!"

Finally after several more moments and no response, she broke. The tears stumbled down her cheeks as the sobs grew louder.

Simon wrapped his arms around her. "Hey, calm down. You have to get a grip, Monica."

Monica's sobs subsided as she gritted her teeth together, "Just so you know, Simon, if Kade is hurt in any way, I will kill Wayne. I don't care if I spend the rest of my life in jail!" She turned and screamed at the door. "I will kill every last one of you if you have hurt my son." She banged fiercely on the door and then dropped to her knees. "He's *gay* for crying out loud; *not a murderer!*"

***

Kade had never considered himself a lucky guy but at
that very second he did.

He had sensed the shot coming and dashed behind one of
the pews just as the bullet zoomed over his head. He
quickly dropped to the floor and crawled forward
underneath the next couple of pews. He was extremely
thankful only the candles were lit at the front of the
sanctuary and that Buddy hadn't turned on any of the lights
when they'd come to pray. It seemed to be a ritual of
theirs—to pray with only candles lit.

Kade froze as he listened to Buddy's footsteps
approaching. He could hear him walking slowly down the
center aisle. Kade quickly scrambled vertical underneath
one of the pews so his feet weren't sticking out.

Kade was certain that Buddy had more bullets in his gun
and he knew the quack wouldn't hesitate to use them either.

He couldn't help but wonder if his father knew what
kind of place this really was. And if he did would he have
still brought him here. As much as it saddened Kade to
admit it, he was sure his dad would have brought him here
regardless. It hurt so much that his dad couldn't love him
for who he was.

Suddenly, Kade saw Buddy's feet two aisles up. He held
his breath, praying that he would walk on by. His heart was
beating so fast, Kade was worried that Buddy might even
hear it. He'd never been this scared before. He suddenly
realized how much he valued his life. He wanted to live so
badly. God had a plan for him, and he was certain he knew
what it was.

Kade was sure he was meant to save other people like
himself from feeling horrible about themselves. He also felt

he was capable of reaching out to those that didn't understand.

Buddy took a couple steps forward and Kade quickly said a prayer. He suddenly wondered if maybe God had plans for him in heaven instead of earth. He had the urge to vomit but choked it down. He never knew that the fear of death could be this frightening.

Buddy stopped in the aisle of the pew that Kade was hidden. Kade saw his feet turn toward him and he was sure that Buddy knew where he was. This was it. His own life flashed before him and he silently started saying the 'Lord's Prayer.'

"I can see you," Buddy said. "Did you really think you could hide from the ones that work for our Father? We are here to honor the Lord and anyone that disrespects him shall be removed from this earth." He tapped the pistol against his palm. "Cindy gave you a chance to redeem yourself. But you still refuse to honor our Father, and I was given permission to kill you if you tried to escape." He laughed a loud, shrewd laugh. "And I don't have a problem doing so."

Suddenly a loud banging silenced him. Everything grew quiet.

Kade listened. There it was again. Someone was definitely banging on a door or something. He saw Buddy's feet turn toward the sound. Kade was sure that Buddy was questioning the noise too.

Kade knew he had to make a quick decision that could affect the rest of his life. He could lie there and wait to be shot, or he could take a chance and run for his life and hope that the distraction scared Buddy enough not to shoot.

The banging came again. This time it was louder and more desperate. This was his only chance. He rolled from under the pew and jumped to his feet. His heart seemed to be caught in his throat and his legs suddenly seemed frozen. He knew this was it!

***

Monica was so upset. She could hear other vehicles pulling up and car doors slamming. But her only thought was for Kade and what was happening to him.

Simon pulled her to her feet. "Come on, Monica. You have to be strong—for Kade." He glanced toward the reporters climbing out of their cars and setting up equipment. "Let's go check to see if there are any other doors?"

Monica cleared her throat. "You're right. I'm sorry." She grabbed Simon's hand and trotted around the side of the building. "We got to find a way inside."

They quickly spotted the back door and Simon tugged on the doorknob but it was also locked.

"Damn it," Monica shrieked.

Simon's eyes scanned the building. "Look, there's an open window." He pointed to a window pushed up a few inches at the far end of the building.

"Thank God!" Monica threw her hands up to the sky before running toward the window. She could hear Simon right at her heels.

Simon easily pushed the window up further and boosted Monica up on the ledge. She quickly pulled herself through and waited for Simon to slide in.

The building was dark and Monica couldn't see a thing in front of her. She wondered how they could possibly find Kade. She sighed with relief as Simon pulled a small pencil-like flashlight out of his pocket and flipped it on. "I am so glad you thought of that. I left mine on Wayne's desk," she whispered.

Simon moved quietly toward the door. "Luckily, I have always carried this with me because it's a screw driver too."

Monica followed Simon quietly down the halls. She couldn't quit thinking about the shot she'd heard earlier. She feared she was going to find Kade in a pool of blood somewhere.

She didn't know how she could ever go on living if Kade was dead. He was her life. Monica's two children were the reasons she climbed out of bed every morning. She couldn't imagine life without either one of them. Since the day she gave birth to Kade, she knew her perception of life had changed, and there wasn't anything she wouldn't do for him.

Simon continued to push doors open as they viewed in the empty rooms.

Monica was certain the building was hazardous; the ceilings looked like they could collapse at any time. Most of the rooms were completely empty except for the kitchen. It was set up like someone actually lived in the building, which made Monica cringe.

"Look!" She pointed toward a light coming from underneath a door.

"Be quiet," Simon whispered as he moved toward the glow. "Maybe you should wait here."

"No way," she said. "I'm coming with you." She tiptoed silently to the door behind Simon.

Suddenly, a loud cry came from behind the door. "Help me!"

"Omigod!" She knew the voice. It was Kade. "It's my baby."

Simon brought his finger to his lips. "Shhh." He pulled out the pistol and quietly opened the door.

Monica's jaw dropped as she witnessed the scene in front of her. Kade was standing near a pew and a stout guy was pointing a gun at him. The room was set up like a sanctuary with pews. A podium stood at the front with candles burning on a nearby table.

The armed guy suddenly spotted Simon and Monica and instantly turned the gun toward them. "Who are you?" he screamed.

Kade suddenly ran toward the front of the room and ducked behind the podium.

Buddy swung the gun back and forth between the podium and Monica and Simon. He moved toward the podium. "The devil can't escape from me." He glanced back over his shoulder. "Leave us alone. I have the Lord's work to do."

Monica knew that the room was too dim for the guy to see Simon's pistol. She glanced toward the window. Sirens could be heard in the distance.

"Mom, get out of here," Kade screamed from behind the podium. "He will kill us all." He poked his head from around the podium. "Oh, God, I love you. I knew you'd find me. But please leave now."

Monica rushed toward Kade but quickly froze when the man turned the gun toward her. "Stop—I'll shoot."

Simon quickly jumped in front of her and pointed his pistol toward the guy. "I can play this game too. And only one of us will live!"

Monica's adrenaline rocketed. She could hear the sirens now growing closer, and she was sure the police would be there within minutes. If only Simon could stall the guy until they got there.

Monica could tell the guy's uneasiness was increasing with every second. He glanced toward the sound of the sirens and the podium. Then he turned his hear toward Simon as if he was debating all his options. Suddenly he shouted at Simon, "Kill me if you must." He turned toward the podium. "But I have to obey our Father's command and kill the demons that are destroying our world." He glanced toward the ceiling as if he was talking to God.

"No," Monica screamed. She tried to rush past Simon but his grip on her shoulder was too tight.

Simon suddenly spoke in a calmer manner to the guy. "Wait! You don't want to do that. The police are here and they will arrest you. You will be locked up for the rest of your life."

The guy glanced back over his shoulder as if he was half-way listening to Simon. He glanced toward the ceiling and mumbled a language that Monica didn't recognize and then he said in a pleading voice, "I don't want to go to jail, Lord."

Simon continued, "God will forgive you. He doesn't want you to go to jail, either. It's okay—really; just put the gun down and everything will be okay."

Monica held her breath as she waited for the man to respond. The guy's face clouded over as if he heard other voices in his head. She was thankful that Simon had thought to use psychology on the senseless fellow.

The guy shook his head vigorously. "I can't. Cindy will be furious." Suddenly tears oozed down his cheeks. "Oh, she will be so mad."

"No, she won't. Cindy wouldn't want you to go to jail. You'd be doing the right thing."

"No," he roared. He ran to the podium. "You might as well come out from behind there."

187

Kade stepped out from behind the podium and squeezed his eyes shut.

Simon rushed to the front of the room, keeping his gun pointed at the guy. "If you pull that trigger, I will have to shoot you." He paused. "You want to die today?"

Monica was on the verge of screaming and running toward Kade, but Simon had the guy's attention again.

The guy glanced back at Simon and then up at the ceiling. Finally after the longest moment, the guy dropped his gun and fell to his feet. "Forgive me, Father. I am weak but I don't want to die yet. Please forgive me." He buried his face into his hands and sobbed.

"Thank you, Lord," Monica moaned as she ran toward Kade. She wrapped her arms around her son and squeezed him with all of her might. She'd never been so thankful in her life.

She knew, at that very moment, that it was God that had saved her son, and she would always be grateful to him for sparing his life.

Chapter Twenty

Kade couldn't stop the tears. He'd never been so scared in his life. Not just for himself but for his mom and Simon too. He knew Buddy had been serious about killing him and the nut had almost succeeded. Fortunately, God must have had other plans for him.

Kade pushed away from his mom and held her at arm's length, "Thank you mom for loving me for who I am." A loud sob escaped from his throat, "Dad did this to me."

"I know, honey. I am so sorry."

Simon kept the gun pointed at Buddy. "You two go on outside. I will stay here and wait for the police." He handed her the flashlight.

"Okay, be careful." Monica held Kade's hand tightly as she led him down the hall. "I know where the front door is now. We passed it earlier."

Suddenly Kade stopped. His whole body was trembling. "We need to hurry before Cindy and Marion get here."

Monica paused in front of the door. "Honey, it's okay. The police will be here any minute and there are over a dozen reporters outside." She unlocked the door. "They are all going to want to talk to you. If you want I will do all the talking—just stay close behind me."

Kade shook his head. "No, Mom. I want to speak my mind. I have so much to say. I want the world to hear me. Please let me talk to them."

"You're not too upset?"

"No, I have to do this."

"Okay." She kissed his cheek and pulled the door open.

Kade had to squint from all of the flashes blinding him. The chaos immediately started. Questions were being thrown at him in every direction.

Monica stopped in front of Dana. "I think he wants to do an interview now."

Dana's eyes lit up. "Awesome." She nodded to her cameraman that she was ready. "Kade, are you ready?"

"Very much so!" He wiped at his nose as a nearby lady quickly handed him a tissue.

Dana immediately started talking into the camera about Kade's disappearance and how Monica had figured out where her son was. "I am here now with Kade who has just been rescued from this building where he has been kept captive." She glanced toward Kade, "Kade, I know you are terribly upset but can you tell us what has happened to you since the last time you saw your mother?"

Kade cleared his throat. He didn't realize how hard this would be. He felt so emotional. "I was kidnapped by my dad." He paused as he choked back the tears, but it was impossible. He couldn't control the tears any more than he could control how much his heart was hurting. "Ummm, my own father did this to me. I am gay, and because of this, my father thought I was an evil person. Like many others in this world, my dad *assumed* that I chose to be gay. He

190

thought that these people, which I believe are a part of a religious cult, could change my sexuality."

He glanced toward the cop cars pulling up. His mother motioned for him to continue as she walked toward the policemen to point them in the right direction. "He tricked me into believing that he had accepted me for who I was." He glanced down at the ground. It hurt just to admit what his father had done to him. He turned back toward the camera. "I will never forget the feeling I had when I thought he still loved me." Kade no longer cared about the tears or how anyone perceived him. "See, I have always tried to please my parents in everything I've done because I knew I was in charge of everything in my life except for this one little thing. I couldn't change my sexuality." He shook his head, "Believe me America, if I could have changed, I would have because I never, ever wanted to disappoint my mom or dad. I loved them so much." He was sobbing again and his voice grew louder. "After a couple of years, I finally accepted myself as a homosexual and I came to terms with it." He glanced toward his mom, knowing the tears streaming down her cheeks were caused by the pain he'd endured. His eyes shifted back toward the camera. "I remember talking to God a lot during this time. I did a lot of praying. And it was through God that I learned to accept the person that I am today. I truly believed once I explained my situation to my parents, they would understand."

Kade's eyes rested back on his mother. "And my mother did. She has the biggest heart ever. I love her so much." He smiled at his mom.

Dana shook her head. "But your father never did accept it?"

"Never! He even divorced my mother because I was gay." He wiped at his nose with the tissue. "So you can image the excitement when I thought he had accepted me for who I was." He shook his head and stared into the night as he waited for the emotion to pass. He glanced back at the camera. "The whole time he had planned on taking me to this horrible place." He glared at the building.

Dana motioned her men around so they could angle in on the building. "Do you feel like telling us your experiences inside that place?" She gestured toward the building.

His mother stepped forward. "Kade, you don't have to talk about this if you're not ready."

He had already seen the police bring out Buddy. He was handcuffed and led to a police car. Two of the officers had jumped into the car and pulled off with him. He imagined the other police were still hanging around, waiting for him to finish his interview. "No, I'm fine." He looked back at the camera. "I need to warn others that are like me about these sorts of people. There are haters out there—that hate homosexuals just because we exist; because we are different."

Kade's voice quivered, "They said I was working for the devil and that God didn't like me. They made me pray all the time." He stopped—the emotion was overwhelming, remembering the way he was treated. "They waxed the hair off my legs and chest for punishment." He heard some of the other reporters gasp. He glanced toward his mother— she was weeping again. He hated to see her cry, but he wanted the world to know how these people had treated him just because he was gay. He stared back at the camera. "They made me say horrible things about myself and made me ask God to forgive me. If I didn't do what they asked, they wouldn't give me anything to eat. They kept me in a dark room with no windows." He squeezed his eyes shut—the horrible memories were still so fresh. He forced his eyes open and his voice grew loud. "I was treated like a criminal because I was born different." He glared into the camera. "No one understands! I am one of many that are born gay. And because of that—we are made fun of, bullied, and treated like we haven't got a soul. This has been going on for years." The tears rolled off his cheeks but he didn't care. His anger was increasing by the second. "Teenagers are killing themselves because they are treated unfairly because of their sexuality." He glanced at Dana and tried to smile. "I am human. I want to be loved just like the next person. I want to have a family just like you do." He glared into the cameras as his voice grew louder, "I *am* not a monster! I *do* have feelings too. I just want people to accept me for who I am—that's all. That's all I ever wanted in this world!"

Dana's eyes watered. "Kade, I am sorry for what you have gone through." She shook her head. "No one deserves to be treated the way you have. I know you're terribly upset and I appreciate you taking the time to talk to me. Do you have any final words to add?"

Kade embraced his mother as he bawled like a baby. He pulled away from her as Dana pushed the microphone in front of his lips. "I do have one last thing to say." He stared into the camera. "Dad, if you're watching this—I want you to know that I loved you so much and tried so hard to make you proud of me." His sobs continued. "Why, Dad? Why did you do this to me? Why couldn't you just love me the way I am?" He bowed his head as he tried to gain his composure. Suddenly, he lifted his head and spoke directly into the camera. "I hate you for doing this to me, Dad. And I will never ever forgive you for this." He nodded toward

Dana. "That's all." He followed his mother out of the camera's view, although cameras were still flashing in every direction. He hugged his mom. "Thank you, Mom for everything. And thank you for loving me and accepting for the person I am. That means the world to me, and one day I will make people understand."

Monica squeezed Kade. "I know you will, sweetie. I am so proud of you already. I couldn't have asked for a better son." She rubbed his back. "I was so worried about you."

"I know. I was so scared too."

More reporters started throwing out more questions, but a nearby officer approached them and led them away from the crowd "I'm sorry to intrude, but I need to talk with both of you. There's also an ambulance on its way so you can get medical attention."

"I am fine, physically," Kade said. "I'm just an emotional wreck right now, but I can talk with you, anyway."

Kade and his mom followed the officer back to his car. "Could you excuse me for just a moment?"

The officer and Monica exchanged puzzled looks. "Sure," the policeman said.

Kade needed a moment of silence. He still hadn't had a chance to let everything sink in. He was still shocked that he had even been rescued.

He walked to the back of the vehicle and bowed his head. He hadn't even had time to thank God for saving him from the dreadful ordeal. Kade knew this was going to be extremely hard to recover from but he knew that God would give him the strength he needed to continue on and make a difference in others life. He was certain that this experience was meant to be, so it would have a huge impact on others. He was certain what God's plan was for him now and he had every intention of making sure it happened.

Chapter Twenty-One

Five Years Later
Friday, May 18, 2013

Monica turned down the radio so she could think about her presentation while she drove to the local high school. She glanced at her watch—she was running right on time. Kade and Luke should be there already. She knew she could count on them to have everything set up by the time she got there for the assembly.

She thought about how far they'd come in the last five years since Kade's kidnapping. She always thought everything always happened for a reason and now she was certain of it.

After that emotional interview from Kade the night he was rescued, everything changed. The interview went nationwide and had touched so many people. Kade was asked to be on a half-dozen TV shows. His story hit newspapers all over the country. Monica couldn't believe how much attention his story had gotten. And it paid off because it really helped their programs take off. Now *John's Law Forums* were being formed all over the country. Their programs were being presented in over 32 states and consistently growing.

Monica ended up retiring from teaching and spent all her time working with LGBT organizations all over the nation. She had over 185 volunteers' nationwide working with her.

It seemed after Kade's incident, homosexuality started being viewed differently. Now over 24 states had legalized same-sex marriage and Monica figured in a couple more years they would all be legalized. Kansas wasn't one of the fortunate ones yet, but she was sure it was just a matter of time. Finally, the world was starting to learn the truth about homosexuals. And just to think Kade helped make it happen made her so proud.

She briefly thought of Wayne. She didn't like to waste positive energy thinking about negative people, but she knew Wayne would be getting out of prison next year. She couldn't help but wonder how he would play a part in his kids' lives. She knew Kade would never have anything to do with him. She figured Karmen would want him back in her life. After all, they had kept contact the last five years through letters. Despite what she wanted to happen, she knew her children were now adults and could rightfully make their own decisions.

She thought of Simon and how fortunate she was to have him. She had married him three years ago and hadn't had a second doubt about it since. He was an amazing man and supported all of her work. He never complained about her late hours or the meals that didn't get cooked. He knew how much her work meant to her.

She pulled into an empty parking space at the school, gathered her material, and stuck them into her brief case. She'd always end the year by putting on an assembly for the local high school and Kade and Luke always took time away from their work to help.

Kade finished college in Arizona but had returned back home to Olathe after he graduated. Monica was glad that Luke had remained in Kade's life while he was in college. They had taken turns flying back and forth to see each other. Since Kade's return home, they had been living together for the last year. They talked about getting married as soon as the same sex marriage law passed.

Kade ran a music store and just recently he helped Luke open up his own bakery. They were both doing well with their businesses.

Now if she could get Karmen through her last couple years of college, maybe her life would calm down. She was glad that Karmen had decided to go to a nearby community college. She smiled silently—now if she'd just decide her major.

Monica locked the car and headed inside the school. She strolled into the gym. She knew exactly where to go since she'd been coming here the last five years. The boys had already set up the table with the brochures and flyers.

Monica gave them each a hug and thanked them for coming.

The lively bunch of kids were escorted into the gym and the chatter and laughter could be heard in every direction. Finally, the principal told them to quiet down. He introduced Monica, Kade and Luke.

Kade started his story about John and then told about what his own dad had done to him five years ago. He spoke about how he managed to pull himself up and go on with life. Luke gave the statistics on the gay community within the country.

Monica finished up by praising anybody who is different and explaining that they shouldn't be ashamed of who they were. After she finished her speech, she asked for questions.

A freckled, red hair boy stood up and announced he was gay. Monica had witnessed this before in prior assemblies and wasn't surprised by it. She especially loved the sound of applause after he announced it. She knew bullying was no longer as big of an issue as it used to be, and there was a zero tolerance ordinance for it. Seven more kids took turns standing up and announcing they also had homosexual feelings. Each time, the other kids would applaud and make positive comments about it being no big deal.

But it was the chubby dark haired girl that really got Monica's attention.

The girl glanced nervously around the gym before she made her announcement. "Hi. My name is Stacy. I know that I am attracted to women." She stared down at the ground briefly and then back toward Monica. "But for me it is harder. My parents would not accept me as a lesbian. If they found out, I would be kicked out of my home."

Monica had heard the story before and her heart broke for these kids. "I know it is the older generation that has the most issues with homosexuality," she said. "And every one of you in this room has the power to make positive changes and help others see differently." She rested her hands on her hips. "Let me ask you this. Can any of your parents help you with your Algebra?" Monica heard a ton of no's, along with giggles. "How about your computers—do they help you with all of your technical problems?"

A boy shouted out, "Shoot, my parents don't even know how to turn on one."

Stacey spoke again, "My mother won't even touch my computer. She's scared she'll break it." The kids all laughed and agreed with her.

"Exactly," Monica said. "And do you know why?"

The room grew silent as they waited for Monica to continue.

"Because all of you are more educated than your parents are—education is way more advanced now than it was when your parents went to school." She glanced around the room, giving them time to digest this information. "And all of you now are more educated on homosexuality than your parents are. When they went to school, gays were scared to talk about their sexual preferences...so they hid it. Many of them went through life never coming out of the closet." Monica shook her head. "And as sad as it is—it is true. Many homosexuals have led secret lives never telling anyone their secret. Many people have died never getting to explore their true feelings for love. Instead, many chose never to marry or some would marry the opposite sex just to cover up their identity. It was definitely a much harder life for gays when your parents were growing up than it is now." She paused. "And since then, your parents *still* haven't been educated on it. All they know is that it is something you don't talk about and that you should be ashamed of it. See, education on homosexuality never existed for them and no one has ever told them any differently about it."

Monica took a sip of her water. "This is how each and every one of you can make a difference. You don't have to be gay, bisexual, or a lesbian to educate your parents on it. The more you and I can reach out and teach others, the more the issue will be accepted in our country." Applause filled the room and Monica was certain she had gotten her point across. "Everything we have talked about today, I have information on that I would like to pass out to all of you. And when you get home tonight, if you could just take five minutes to tell your parents about your day and maybe show them the brochures that you picked up, I would be grateful. You possibly could teach your parents something they weren't aware of!" She pointed around the room. "It is all of you—the younger generation that has the power to change this world and make it a better place for us all to live in. Right now *you* hold the future of our country in your hands and *you* can make a difference." More applause and yelps passed through the room. Monica knew she had succeeded today in delivering her message.

She thanked the kids, the principal, and the teachers for their time and then wrapped the assembly up by having the teachers hand out the brochures.

She gave Kade and Luke a hug and thanked them for their help. As she walked to her car, she smiled silently; she knew the day had been a huge success. Every time she had a good assembly, she knew she was one step closer in bringing unity to this world.

She was seeing more and more homosexuals showing affection in public. The other day while she was at the mall, two guys were walking arm in arm. Not one person turned to stare at them like they did at Crystal and her five years ago. She knew the world was changing—and in a good way.

All she wanted when she left this earth was not to worry about her kids and know that they were happy with their lives.

Every day for the last five years, Monica had been worried about Kade. She was concerned that the past had left a scar on him for life.

But now she knew it had actually made him a better person. He had started many different clubs for gays in college, and he was truly proud of who he was.

She stopped outside her car and glanced toward the sky, "Thank you, God, for giving me such a loving gay Christian son." She climbed into her car. She knew that her job was done as far as raising Kade. She knew now that he would survive no matter what obstacles he had to cross.

***

Wednesda, July 3, 2013

Kade saddled up Maggie Mae and jumped on her. "Come on, girl. Let's go." He gave her a nudge. He knew she understood him and that there was no need to shout at her or kick her. She didn't move as quite as fast as she used to, but she still got excited every time Kade put a saddle on her. It was as if she knew exactly where they were going.

Kade hadn't got to ride much when he went off to college but he did make it a point to come and ride every time he came back to visit. In the last year that he moved back to Olathe, he'd come to ride quite often. Every once in awhile, Luke would come with him, but he didn't enjoy it as much as Kade did.

He rode silently up to his favorite spot—the waterfall. It was a beautiful day. The sunflowers were in bloom, the birds were chirping, and the weather couldn't be more perfect. It had to be his favorite time of the year to ride.

Kade reached his spot and slid quietly off of Maggie Mae. He led her to drink before tying her up to the tree. He reached in his pocket and pulled out a sugar cube. He laid it flat in his hand for Maggie Mae to lick up. He patted her on the head. "See, I know the sugar cubes are the real reason you like going with me, girl." He chuckled to himself.

He walked over to the waterfall and let the sound of it soothe his mind. He stared at the falling water for several moments, enjoying the fresh air that filled his lungs.

Sometimes, when he was here alone, his mind would wander back to those horrible days he'd been with the trio in that hideous place. At the trial, the truth was discovered about them. Cindy, Buddy and Marion were in some kind of cult with Cindy being the lead ringer. It turned out that Cindy had convinced Buddy and Marion to follow her command. They'd already pocketed thousands of dollars from innocent people. There were still victims coming forward. Kade was thrilled that they'd be in jail for a long time and couldn't hurt any more people.

His dad's lawyer tried to argue that Wayne was convinced that they were a respectable religious group, or he wouldn't have taken his son there.

Kade fought back the tears—his father had still thought he hadn't done anything wrong. Of course, the prosecutor nailed him. *You can't kidnap your son and send him to people like he's a dog that needed trained.*

Kade picked up a rock and threw it into the creek. He didn't think he'd ever be able to forgive his father. To this day, his father still hadn't apologized for what he'd done. His dad hadn't even look at him in the courtroom.

Sometimes, childhood memories bothered Kade. He still had reminiscences of the fun times him and his father had while he was growing up.

Kade had learned over the last few years that some people are so set on the way they believe and are so

203

narrow-minded that they don't want to listen to reason from anyone. He figured it was the way they were brought up.

It was sad to think there were so many people out there that would rather hate and not know the truth than accept the truth and be compassionate toward the LGBT community.

He shrugged and strolled over to the edge of the path. He knelt down next to the wooden cross he had built. He stared at the words he'd carved on it, *My Beloved Friend, John, July 3, 2008.*

He couldn't believe it had been five years since John ended his life. Kade had made a point to come to this very spot every year on the date of John's death.

He recalled how John had loved this place and how it had been the only place in the world that he'd felt at peace. Kade always felt closer to John when he came here.

He always remembered the last time they spent here together and the secrets they had shared with each other. He recalled how John didn't like himself and how he'd longed to be straight.

Kade stood and closed his eyes. He spoke out loud, "John, I know you never felt worthy and didn't think too highly of yourself. I, for one, thought very highly of you, and you were the best friend I have ever had." He knelt back down. "If only you knew that because of you the whole country has changed.

He paused to gather his thoughts. "I was devastated when you committed suicide, and I wanted to help others that were like you to accept the way they were. I wanted people to understand that we never chose to be gay." Kade's eyes watered. "And the way I have done that is by sharing your story. So because of you, John, many people have changed their views on judging others."

Kade flicked away a tear. "The world is a much better place to live than what it used to be." He paused. "Oh, don't get me wrong, we have a ways to go—but I know it is going to happen soon, and I just really wished you could have stuck around to witness it."

Kade pulled out a rainbow flag, a symbol for gay pride, out of his back pocket and stuck it next to the other four in the ground. "I truly believe if you were alive today, you would proudly accept this flag. You are missed so much. I will never forget you, my dear friend."

Kade knew John wouldn't be the last gay to kill himself. There had been many since John's death, and he knew there would still be others in the future that couldn't accept the way God intended them to be. But if he could save even one teenager from committing suicide, then all the work him and his mother had done would have been worth it.

Kade stood and gazed around him. He remained perfectly still—just letting the serenity of the forest consume him.

Finally, he climbed back on Maggie Mae and galloped into the sunset. He glanced one last time over his shoulder at the five rainbow flags blowing in the wind and suddenly he had an overwhelming feeling that John was truly okay now and finally at peace.

THE END

Author's Note

Although this is a fictional story, gay teens commit suicide every day. I wrote this novel in order to bring awareness to all the children, teens, and even adults that are being bullied across the country.

I think we are long past due for a change. This country needs to quit taking baby steps and do some major reconstruction to change the way the LGBT community is viewed.

It concerns me that teenagers are taking their own lives because of the way they are treated in society because of their sexual orientation.

This is so wrong and needs to be addressed by every one of us. We all need to step up and do our part to save these depressed and confused teenagers.

First, we need to educate those that don't understand the gay lifestyle. We need to emphasize that these people do not choose their sexuality.

It seems to me that a lot of the older generation has never been educated on homosexuality. All they know is what their parents told them when they were growing up. We are far more educated on people's differences now than they were years ago, and we need to keep educating those that have no clue.

We need to accept the LGBT community as part of our society. We need to teach our children to accept homosexuals in their schools and teach them not to ridicule or bully them.

I believe we could do this by having assemblies or workshops that touch this issue. There are many different things that could be done to introduce the gay lifestyle. For example: Literature class—rather than banning books because they deal with the topic of homosexuality, we could incorporate it into high school studies and form topics about the characters.

The more we teach our children that this is something natural, the more likely the bulling would cease. This would also help more teenagers come out of the closet because they wouldn't feel so ashamed.

I have heard about churches that have actually kicked homosexuals out of to their church service. I am appalled! How could any church discriminate against anyone that wants to worship the Lord?

Discrimination needs to be a thing of the past. It is time for all of us to finally unite and live peacefully as one.

Civil rights taught us to accept one another regardless of the color of our skin. So why can't we learn to accept each other based off what's within our skin?

Here are some of the statistics I got off of the Trevor Project website:

In the United States, more than 34,000 people die by suicide each year (Centers for Disease Control and Prevention, CDC 2007).

Suicide is the third leading cause of death among 15 to 24-year-olds, accounting for over 12% of deaths in this age group; only accidents and homicide occur more frequently (National Adolescent Health Information 2006).

Lesbian, gay, and bisexual youth are up to four times more likely to attempt suicide than their heterosexual peers (Massachusetts Youth Risk Survey 2007).

LGB youth who come from highly rejecting families are more than 8 times as likely to have attempted suicide than LGB peers who reported no or low levels of family rej ection (Ryan C, Huebner D, et al - Peds 2009;123(1):346-352).

Nine out of 10 LGBT students (86.2%) experienced harassment at school; three-fifths (60.8%) felt unsafe at school because of their sexual orientation; and about one-third (32.7%) skipped a day of school in the past month because of feeling unsafe (GLSEN National School Climate Survey 2009).

It is estimated that between 20 and 40 percent of all homeless youth identify as lesbian, gay, bisexual, and/or transgender (2006 National Gay & Lesbian Task Force: An Epidemic of Homelessness). 62% of homeless LGB youth will attempt suicide at least once—more than two times as many as their heterosexual peers (Van Leeuwen JMm et al – Child Welfare 2005)

* For more information, groups like the Gay Lesbian and Straight Education Network (GLSEN), Parents, Families and Friends of Lesbians and Gays (PFLAG), and The Trevor Project have been working to educate the public on this issue and to stop these unnecessary tragedies.

www.ingramcontent.com/pod-product-compliance
Lightning Source LLC
Chambersburg PA
CBHW031334170626
46807CB00002B/692